THE WRATH
of
GOD

THE WRATH
of
GOD

JIM BALZOTTI

CREATION
HOUSE

THE WRATH OF GOD: A NOVEL by Jim Balzotti
Published by Creation House
A Charisma Media Company
600 Rinehart Road
Lake Mary, Florida 32746
www.charismamedia.com

Unless otherwise noted, all Scripture quotations are from the King James Version of the Bible.

Design Director: Justin Evans
Cover design by Ampersand Graphics, Stuart, FL

This is a work of fiction. Names, places, characters and incidents are either the product of the author's imagination or are used fictitiously, and any resemblance to actual persons, living or dead, events or locales is entirely coincidental.

Visit the author's website: www.wrathofgodthebook.com.

Library of Congress Control Number: 2015952363
International Standard Book Number: 978-1-62998-502-2
E-book International Standard Book Number:
978-1-62998-503-9

First edition

16 17 18 19 20 — 987654321
Printed in the United States of America

*To my children, Amy, Jeff, and Mike,
who gave my life love and meaning.*

*To my grandchildren, Adriana
and Domenic, and my expected
grandson, who have given me
new wonder and amazement.*

*And to the memory of my parents,
Domenic and Marie, who instilled
faith and love in my heart.*

And I looked, and behold a pale horse: and his name that sat on him was Death, and Hell followed with him. And power was given unto them over the fourth part of the earth, to kill with sword, and with hunger, and with death, and with the beasts of the earth…

And they cried with a loud voice, saying, How long, O Lord, holy and true, dost thou not judge and avenge our blood on them that dwell on the earth?…

And, lo, there was a great earthquake; and the sun became black as sackcloth of hair, and the moon became as blood…

For the great day of his wrath is come; and who shall be able to stand?

—REVELATION 6:8, 10, 12, 17

ACKNOWLEDGMENTS

MY IMMENSE GRATITUDE to my two dear friends Alexis Nakos and Donna Buendo, who edited, and edited, and edited this book. Both are brilliant and accomplished women.

To my college friend Christopher White Webster, recently retired from the State Department, who gave me insight into the potential dangers of America's economic dependence on China and elsewhere.

Thank you, Allen Quain of Creation House, for your guidance and encouragement.

—JIM BALZOTTI

FOREWORD

HARDLY A DAY passes without something occurring that illustrates the interdependence of the world's inhabitants on each other. Developments and events in one country can have consequences far beyond its boundaries. Those consequences affect the country and the developments or events which initially prompted the reaction elsewhere. Also, history teaches us that decisions and events influence future developments often when no relationship exists between them.

When Republican Party members in Congress and President Obama and his fellow Democratic Party members in Congress were at loggerheads over the shape and amount of the US government budget and the level of US government debt in 2013, Jim Balzotti asked me what would happen if China, which holds a significant share of the US government's debt, were to request immediate repayment. In answering his question, I had no idea that our conversation would cause him to write the gripping and provocative narrative that follows. While this narrative is strictly a work of fiction, a scenario along the lines presented is not completely outside the realm of possibility. The story also prompts the reader to think about issues human beings have grappled with for centuries such as religion's role in a society's functioning, whether divine influence shapes events, and the appropriate mix of self-reliance and government assistance in determining human actions. There are no clear-cut answers to these questions, but I believe they are critical to consider carefully in making decisions about proposed actions.

I hope that readers of this book will find it as well written and thought provoking as I have.

—Christopher W. Webster
Chief, Developed Country Trade Division
Bureau of Economic and Business Affairs
Department of State (Retired)

PROLOGUE

T HE YEAR IS 2028 and the world is at war.

After years of deficit spending and government paralysis that led to the devaluation of its currency and widespread riots, the United States suffered a complete collapse of its government and has been conquered militarily by China.

Religion has been outlawed upon penalty of death. Martial law has been instituted, with hundreds of thousands of Americans put in detention zones on starvation rations.

All forms of media are now prohibited, and the main computer junctions controlling the Internet have been destroyed.

Small bands of well-armed militias are resisting, with death squads of highly trained Chinese military units hunting them down. Public executions are common.

China, with its smaller vassals North Korea, Venezuela, and Pakistan, launched a bold move to attain world domination, crushing any nation that does not surrender unconditionally.

Fall 2024

WASHINGTON DC

THE WAR BETWEEN China and the United States did not begin with a single gunshot, troops invading, or bombs exploding.

It began with a simple request.

The People's Republic of China had lent to the United States over a period of decades nineteen trillion dollars, and China wanted it back. *All of it. Now.*

Requests like this, although hardly the norm, were always made through back channels and then only through senior diplomats in hushed tones with a great deal of formality. Perhaps over tea, but not this time. This was a well-thought-out, planned strategy by Chairman Chang. He wanted the world's attention. Before the president was even notified, China leaked the request publically to every major news organization across the globe. Wall Street, which always reacted to rumors, plunged 580 points. Trading was halted. Talk radio hosts were flooded with calls from a panicking public, not quite sure what to make of it. Some callers angrily declared we should just not pay the Chinese and tell them to go pound sand up their butts. Almost all agreed it was the politicians' fault for their liberal, wasteful spending patterns. Ambassadors from countries around the world called their counterparts in Washington trying to get any kind of response in order to gauge how such an event might affect their own countries. All other global news took a backseat to this new development. The Chinese had strategically contrived a tipping point in world history.

Of course the United States did not have the money. Not a tenth of it. Not a hundredth of it. Not if you counted all the gold in Fort Knox. Decades of uncontrolled wasteful spending, along with an inability of politicians in Congress to either curb spending or put deficit reduction measures into place, risked plunging the United States into a fiscal black hole without the possibility of recovery. The result was an economy strangled by social programs that the government could not support. It was estimated that a third of the population was paying for the other two-thirds *not* to work. Congress would not raise taxes. Congressional members wanted to be reelected year after year. Raising taxes was a guaranteed ticket to getting thrown out of office. As a result, more money was printed and borrowed excessively. The debt ceiling was raised annually while political bluster reiterated that Washington needed to cut spending. When cutbacks came, it was to the space program, military defense, and government agencies such as the CIA, Homeland Security, FBI, and the NSA. At the same time, foreign aid increased. It took precedence over funding domestic programs such as mental health, veterans, children, and the elderly. The average American could not reconcile the fact that our government had built roads and bridges overseas in hostile foreign lands yet the American people were being told we had no funds to fix our own crumbling infrastructure. The government's mismanagement of Social Security was the most egregious offense. Social Security, funded by American workers, was running out. Constantly mislabeled as an entitlement program, it was in fact a retirement fund paid into by American workers over their working lives. Rather than being held in a separate designated account with a singular purpose, contributions were placed in the general fund, which was treated like a child's piggy bank by politicians and special interest groups who couldn't wait to dip into it with their greedy hands.

The US Navy was at the lowest level since the 1960s; military bases had been closed around the world. The space program was halted and the once proud NASA completely eliminated.

The government's justification for severe military budget cuts was the focus and priority given to an unlikely threat of a terrorist blowing up a plane. In the interim, troops were not allocated to defend US borders that were porous, thus vulnerable. After all, wasn't the world at peace? Were we not the United States, the most influential and powerful nation in the world? History's lessons went unlearned. Arrogance overshadowed the reality of the rise and fall of nations due to incompetence and corruption from within. One needs only to look at England, Spain, Portugal, ancient Rome, and the great civilizations of Egypt as precedence. The Americans were arrogant but most importantly had grown soft. Soft and corrupt. The disciplines of hard work, individual responsibility, and small government were thrown by the wayside. Newly elected politicians moved away from the Constitution written by the Founding Fathers and regarded it as an inconvenient document.

America was ripe for the taking.

When President Mann was made aware of the *request* for the payment in full to China of the nineteen trillion dollars owed, he first thought it was a miscommunication, perhaps one of the many unfounded rumors for which Washington was famous. Everyone knew the United States did not have the money. How could they? It was such an outrageous request, it had to be erroneous. But when Chairman Chang personally contacted the Chief of State, he knew that it was a devastating reality. Chang tersely reiterated his formal written request. Simply put, the United States owed China a great deal of money, and China was calling in the note. Saying what he had to say, Chang abruptly terminated the call. President Mann assumed that this had to do with the grain deal the United States forced onto China during their drought years ago. He would be partially correct. In 2020, China suffered from a severe three-year-long drought. Seeking to buy grain to feed its starving population, China requested partial debt prepayment in order to make grain purchases in the world market. Washington's only proposition was to barter a reduction of the Chinese debt for grain while overvaluing the commodity by 400 percent. It was an attempt to reduce the deficit owed China. America had the Chinese over a barrel with no other option but to accept. It became a shameful chapter in American history. No man or nation forgets the feel of a sharp blade being held to the throat.

The president was notified that the White House switch-board was swamped with calls from persons claiming entitlement and demanding answers. President Mann summoned his Cabinet, the chairman of the Federal Reserve Board, the Attorney General, along with the Secretary of the Treasury, and the chairman of CFIUS, the Committee on Foreign Investments.

"Ladies and Gentlemen: I've spoken to Chairman Chang, who for all practical purposes is now the sole dictator of China. He assures me that the request is most real and has given us one year to come up with the money. That's nineteen *trillion*, folks! He made it crystal clear that this is not an idle threat. We are challenged with a major power move against the United States, and I need to know what, if anything, we can do about it. The world is watching. I would like to hear from each of you in as few words as possible the exact ramifications of this demand. What are our options? We need a strategic position to counter this threat to our economic stability."

"As we all know," Margaret Webb, the chairwoman of the Federal Reserve Board, confirmed, "we do not have the money. Or more accurately, it's merely print on our T-bills, ink on pieces of paper. Chits, if you will. IOUs. And if the Chinese are calling them in, we simply can't pay them. *Maybe* one trillion...tops. China isn't the only country with our T-bills; numerous nations have invested in them to hedge against their own economies. There is no way we can pay them back, in either dollars or gold. If we should just print the money—which quite honestly, Mr. President, we've been doing for some time now rather than implementing austerity measures—we would devalue our own dollar. Think of it in terms of paying ten dollars for a Coke. Our money would become worthless overnight. We can't borrow the money, since we have been borrowing from the Chinese and others all these years. We don't have enough gold in Fort Knox to give them, since we've been selling that off quietly for years to pay off some of our debt. Thank God the public isn't aware of that strategy!"

"What if we don't pay them? Stall them, Margaret?"

"I doubt we could stall them long enough. As for not paying them, not a good idea. They could legally seize our assets worldwide. Embassies, ships, planes, military instillations—and most damning, all the foreign investments we have around the world. Our largest domestic companies have contracts with our government and are heavily invested in China. They could seize all our monetary as well as physical assets. If we appealed it, on what grounds I don't know, and if it ever got as far as the World Court in Hague, we'd lose. Simply put, we borrowed the money. In a word, Mr. President, we are looking at the collapse of the US dollar. If the Chinese have done this by design, it's brilliant. Most of the world's economies are tied to the dollar. Ironically, one that isn't is the yuan. Up until 2005 the Chinese yuan was pegged to our dollar, but it was removed and now floats in a narrow margin around a fixed base rate tied to a small basket of world currencies. It makes you wonder if this move wasn't planned many years ago."

"So what *can* we do?"

"If this demand is credible, they obviously want something. Give them grain, perhaps. In the meantime, begin turning over surplus property to them that no longer has any value to us. Stall them. We're going to lose these assets anyway. They've made advances in their navy, but I think we could negotiate a release of some of our warships in lieu of dollars and..."

"Give them our warships! My God, Margaret! Are you out of your mind? Are we really thinking this?"

"As I said, Mr. President, we have no choice. Let them have a few assorted warships, even a carrier. Don't forget, our standing army is in shambles due to budget cuts; after all, we don't fight wars with soldiers on the ground anymore. We have the largest arsenal of nuclear weapons in the world. Give them the warships and planes. They could never use them against us. It would reduce a small portion of the debt."

"My God, Margaret! What else?"

"Mr. President, what I would propose as the only viable option would also bring our country to her knees."

"What are you thinking?"

"Drastic cuts. To the bone. We would have to eliminate *all* social programs. Welfare, Social Security, Medicare, Medicaid...everything. *Gone.* No money to education, the arts, medical research and development...we would have to cut all government services to the poor, which quite honestly has turned our society over the years into a welfare state. Why should people work when they get paid to stay home? We even mail a check right to their house! All, and I mean all, disability programs have to go. Next we would have to attempt to raise additional money by offering very high interest rates on our T-bills, maybe 8 percent, which in itself is self-defeating. With the dollar in jeopardy of falling and taking Europe and South America's currency with it, who would buy them? We're having a hard time paying the interest on the Chinese loan now, for God's sake! If we raise interest rates, the borrowing rates all rise. Money becomes prohibitively more expensive. It would have a double whammy of us collapsing our own dollar. The cost of gas, food, credit cards, adjustable rate mortgages, rent all skyrocket. People are barely getting by now. The unemployment rate is up to 12.7 percent. It could climb well above 70 percent. What you would be looking at, Mr. President, is a depression that would make 1929 look like a hiccup in the economy. You could expect widespread panic and civil disorder. Mr. President, the Chinese are in a position to collapse the United States from within, and I'm just not sure what you can do to stop it."

"Something else, Mr. President," said Brett Markus. Brett was the head of CFIUS, the Committee on Foreign Investments in the US, an agency that closely monitored and regulated what businesses or strategic property could be sold in the United States to foreign investors. "In the beginning of your first term, Congress relaxed rules on foreign investment and you signed off on it. In addition to the purchase of the Sears Tower, the Trump properties, we also allowed the sale of our largest energy corporation, Unocal, to the Chinese for $18.5 trillion, and Chevron for $11 trillion. They've purchased controlling interests in the Hoover Dam and some smaller hydroelectric plants. Bottom line, our top energy companies can easily be placed in a stranglehold at China's discretion, which in itself poses great national security concerns. A flip of a switch and portions of America go dark."

"Okay. All of you, I need to be alone. Meet back here in one hour."

He thought back to 2016 when he ran for president as the outsider and successful businessman who would bring the much-needed change and a fresh perspective to Washington. His candid and unscripted words spoken from the heart touched many Americans, and although he was well known for his business acumen, and often graced the cover of national magazines and newspapers, he had never run for public office before, let alone the highest office.

He ran as an independent, which in itself had never been done successfully before, but he felt strongly he was an independent, and wanted to be the president for all the people.

He was swept into office with much hope and promise for change, garnering 72 percent of the popular vote, but quickly realized that the Congress and the Senate cared little about enacting policies and laws that would lead America to firmer ground and stability, but instead only cared for their own personal self-interests and petty grievances. Nero playing his fiddle while Rome burned. The massive debt threatened to destroy the country, but the lawmakers were unwilling to work together to prevent the stagecoach from plummeting off the cliff. Now it was too late.

The president sat back in his chair and ran his hand over his balding scalp. At the end of this day he thought he'd be lucky to have any hair left.

Fall 2028

NORTHERN MAINE

MATT OPENED THE weathered, splintered brown door to his small, rustic wood cabin and stepped into the bright October sunshine. He put his arms behind his head to stretch and ease his cramped muscles in his back and shoulders. It's true what they say he thought. It stinks to get old. Although it was still warm, even up here in northern Maine, he felt a chill shake him that made his bones rattle, so he pulled his old, well-worn grey cardigan sweater tighter around his large frame. Maine was basking in the unseasonable warmth of a late Indian summer, but Matt knew that frigid temperatures accompanied by heavy snowfall lay right around the corner. Just the thought of the impending cold caused him to shudder involuntarily. Matt silently admonished himself for being a procrastinator. He knew he had to seal the new cracks in the walls of his cabin before the snow fell, using a mixture of mud and pine needles covered with sap. The truth was, ever since he had that vision as a young boy, he never could get warm enough. Many, many years ago as a child, when his friends wore shorts and ran about bare-chested, he would always wear a light sweater and jeans whenever he went out to play. His mother, having lost Matt's father to a heart attack while he was plowing the fields on the family farm, was not one to spend her limited income by running to a doctor every time Matt was sick or hurt. She just didn't have the extra funds, period. Nevertheless, she grew concerned when Matt constantly complained of being cold, even asking for a blanket on the hottest summer nights. She considered the possibility that he might have a problem with his circulatory system, so she would reluctantly cover him with a down-filled comforter. His mother's concern eventually turned to alarm when his complaints about feeling cold became persistent. He was surprised when she announced that they would be taking the long drive to Bangor. He vividly remembered driving down the coast to the hospital. His mom spent the day sitting in a hard pink plastic chair in the crowded waiting room, drinking acidic lukewarm coffee from the vending machines in the cafeteria while Matt underwent a series of tests. Finally the doctors came out and informed her that they could find nothing wrong with Matt, and suggested that quite possibly he would outgrow it. So home they went. He never did.

Matt picked up his fishing rod off the front porch; it was really nothing more than a sapling cut from a birch tree. He fastened a length of nylon string with a barbed hook attached to it and began to walk to the stream that meandered quietly beyond his cabin. He picked his way through the towering evergreens, mostly spruce and giant pines that were darker and a richer color green than the smaller leaf trees that struggled to get their share of the sun.

Above, a hawk soared around in lazy circles looking for prey, against an azure sky filled with billowy clouds gently pushing east. Matt stopped for a moment, watching the hawk and breathing in the sweet scent of the forest pines. He gave thanks to God for all the wondrous gifts He had given to mankind, and then contemplated the ingratitude of so many. Even before America was overthrown by China, we were using up our God-given natural resources at a breakneck speed. We built super fishing trawlers that depleted the oceans of fish faster than they could reproduce. When the second oil embargo was imposed by OPEC in 2018, we cut obscene cavernous pits in the earth to mine the black coal that lay beneath. The fracking was intensified. Natural gas companies drilled thousands and thousands of holes into the fragile ecosystem, filling them with a mixture of poisonous chemicals in order to release the natural gas that was buried below. The US government, reeling from large-scale protests as a result of the high cost of home heating fuel and gasoline, turned a blind eye toward this environmental nightmare. Congress went as far as scuttling the Clean Water Act passed years prior to stop this exact disaster from happening. Now, too late to correct the permanent damage done, vast tributaries of underground water which once ran sweet and clear were polluted to such a point they were unfit to drink. That, of course, spiked a run on clean water, a condition exploited by major corporations buying and controlling the remaining supply. The corporations first pollute the water supply and subsequently take over what was remaining of the clean water and sell it to the public, who had no choice but to buy it at a usurious rate. He would smile at the irony if it wasn't so excruciatingly painful. Of course, now China controlled all of America's natural resources, diminished as they were. So it was a moot point.

Matt walked along the broken shoreline and picked his way through the fallen branches and massive boulders strewn about to reach an ancient sunken pine tree, lying half in and half out of the water. This was his favorite fishing spot. He knew from growing up in Maine and fishing with his dad that fat speckled rainbow trout like to hide beneath the surface and pounce on any juicy bugs that might fall from the overhanging tree limbs into their domain.

While Matt put a fresh earthworm, twisting and turning, on his hook, he watched three painted box turtles, their shells dark and smooth with a faint orange stripe sunning themselves on a nearby rock. Green dragonflies, slender and elegant, lifted off effortlessly from a nearby lily pad. It was always here, being surrounded by the ever-present beauty and wonder of nature, that Matt felt closest to God. Somehow, being in a church, no matter how ornate it was or how melodious the pipe organ played, could not compare to the natural sounds God gave to His world. The songs of the sparrows, the wind whistling through the trees, even the croaking melody of the frogs—it made sense to him. After all, isn't it true that man made the churches but God created the entire world?

Matt turned his face toward the sun, feeling its warmth. He tossed his line along the submerged tree where the summer insects were gathering and buzzing about. The water immediately exploded as a big trout took the worm in its mouth and then tried to dive under the submerged log for safety. Matt expertly allowed the trout to partially swallow the worm before he raised the tip of his pole, setting the hook firmly in its mouth. He coaxed it away from the log, and in one swift motion leaned down and firmly grasped the slippery fish in his hand. He deftly removed the hook and placed his catch in a brown wicker basket attached to his hip, a gift his father had given to him on his eighth birthday. The basket remained one of his most cherished possessions. He thought back to that day, which seemed so long ago, smiling inwardly at the coincidence that today would have marked the opening of fishing season in Maine, a special day he had once looked forward to sharing with his dad. Matt remembered how excited he was to climb into that old red truck and finally be able to go to his dad's favorite fishing hole. He pictured his mother handing them a picnic lunch as Matt and his dad got into the family vehicle, a red four-wheel-drive Ford 150. A pickup truck was almost a necessity if you were going to live in northern Maine, with its tough winters and the mud season that followed. The F-150 was pushing nearly 200,000 miles. When Matt's mom said they should start thinking about buying a new truck, Matt's dad laughed and said it was just getting broken in.

Matt vividly recalled pulling out of the dirt driveway, giving a wave to his mom while changing the radio station from the Christian pop that his father favored to a new rock 'n' roll station out of Bangor. His father just shook his head with amusement.

On that day, his eighth birthday, Matt remembered the signpost peppered with bullet holes that marked the turnoff from the interstate in order to head west on Route 11 through the town of Medway. It was the last town they would pass before the asphalt road would turn to hard packed brown gravel. They were headed north into a remote region of the Allagash Wilderness, a place where no one lived and few people ever visited. A number of years ago companies mined quartz there, but that market dried up in the 1930s, and the area reverted back to a complete wilderness state. It was even too remote for most of the people who were native to Maine. There were no fire or police services, few roads, and instead of town names, there were only faded township numbers painted on a thin, white vertical post sticking out of the ground by the side of the road to indicate your location. Definitely not an area in which to break down or suffer a heart attack. Lacking cell towers, phoning for help in the event of an emergency would be impossible.

They drove slower down the dusty dirt road, hearing the small pebbles bouncing off the sides of the truck, for almost another twenty miles before they pulled into a cutoff in the forest which was almost invisible. Pine branches scraped the doors and windows as the truck meandered right and left, going further down the narrow path until they came to a break in the trees. Matt quickly unbuckled his seat belt and ran around to the bed of the pickup where the fishing rods were stored. He placed his dad's rod against the side of the truck. Unable to control his excitement, he yelled, "I'll meet you there, dad!" and bolted down the path to the lake. His dad smiled and collected his rod and picnic basket as the smell of his wife's honey fried chicken and buttermilk biscuits made him think of things other than fishing.

He walked down the pathway to the lake just in time to watch Matt bait his hook and cast his line into the still water. His own dad, Matt's grandfather, had found this hidden cove on Rainbow Lake when he was just a boy. It became a family secret. It was too far and too difficult to get to for most people. The city slickers would not want to get their shiny new pickups or station wagons scratched up on the branches driving through the trees, and the other locals had their own secret fishing holes.

By the time he put the wicker lunch basket on a branch, out of the reach of ants, and baited his line, Matt was squealing with excitement as his rod bent downward under the weight of the fish now on his hook. Although only eight, Matt was already becoming quite the outdoorsman. He could fish, hunt, start a fire, and build a shelter from the elements if need be. He was his father's son, he thought proudly. Whenever he finished his chores, you could find him exploring in the nearby woods that surrounded the farm. While his father watched, Matt slowly waded into the water, knowing that a quick jerk of the line would usually mean the loss of his prize. He reached down and, using his net, landed a very respectable two-pound brown brook trout. Once safely back on the shore, he held the fish high for his dad to see. With a smile stretching across the lake, Matt christened his new birthday wicker basket by placing his catch in it.

After fishing for two hours, having caught their limit of three trout each, they broke for lunch before heading home. Father and son shared the contents of the picnic basket, eating all the fried chicken and biscuits between them. For dessert, his mom put two crisp apples picked from their own orchard. Matt, still excited over his fishing bounty, bit lustily into the apple, juice spurting down his chin. His dad laughed, wiping Matt's chin with a paper napkin, remembering how his dad did this very same thing for him.

"Son, look around you. God gives us everything we could possibly want. The woods are filled with game to hunt, the streams and lakes teeming with fish to catch, meadows covered with blueberry bushes, fresh water to drink, and firewood to keep us warm. God has given us everything we could possibly need to sustain us, and even gives us the song of the bluebird to serenade us, and all He asks is that we remain faithful and be good stewards of His domain. He gives us simple rules in His Holy Book and words to live by."

Now an adult, Matt had never forgotten those words— although he thought, sadly, the world surely had.

He remembered that fishing trip with his dad, oh so long ago, and the vision he had that day. They had just finished their picnic lunch. The sun was high overhead, and it was hot. His dad had stretched out on the ground, tipped his hat over his face, and told Matt he was going to rest his eyes for a bit. Matt knew what that meant—his dad would no doubt be snoring like a black bear in hibernation in no time. So Matt decided to hike along the lake and do some exploring. Before long he was getting pretty hot, so he decided he'd cool off and go swimming. His father really didn't like him swimming so close to eating a meal, myth or not, but the still water beckoned to him, so he stripped down to his underwear and dived into the cool, blue-green water. He swam around a bit, seeing how far he could go underwater while holding his breath. When he got bored, he walked out of the water onto the shore, sat down, and began to pull on his shorts.

To this day, Matt can't explain what happened next. He heard a voice, but it came from no singular direction. Although at first he couldn't understand what it was saying, he eventually recognized his name. He was hearing "Matthew," something his mother called him when she was really, really angry at him. He sat quietly, and the area immediately surrounding him grew bright with a shimmering white light that was so intense, so blinding, that it should have been hot, but it wasn't.

The voice called out his name again, and he became very still. His body, rather than becoming tense with the fear of the unknown, became very relaxed, as if he went into a hypnotic state.

Matthew, you have been chosen to lead My people to safety upon the day I return. You must remember this place, for it is holy, and it is here you will lead My flock. When the time of the Apocalypse is near, I will give you a sign—the Son of Man will appear in the heavens and upon your body, and you will know as it is written, so shall it come to pass. And all of the tribes of the Earth will see the Son of Man and shall tremble as with great power He will cleanse the Earth of its wickedness.

Matt could hear the voice in his head, but it was unlike any sound he had heard before. The sound was soft but clear. It penetrated his consciousness but originated from within. A spiritual presence, wonderful and joyous, filled his body. He sat quietly listening, but at that moment became aware that while the voice was speaking to him, all other sounds of the woods had ceased. Everything became very still. Once the voice stopped, he could hear the sounds of a nearby brook babbling as it made its way into the lake, as well as all the other myriad sounds of the forest. He watched a gaggle of geese pass overhead, silhouetted against the cloudless blue sky. A summer rain appeared magically, sprinkling tiny drops over the petals of the wildflowers, and just as suddenly stopped, leaving the forest fresh and renewed.

At the time of the vision, Matt was overwhelmed with a terrible sense of futility, and at first sensed he was on the brink of death. His whole body ached with an inner cold that would plague him for many years. That feeling gave way to one of crystal clarity, a revelation and a deep understanding that God wanted him to be strong, and that He had a purpose for him.

Matt always attended church regularly with his parents. After Mass ended he enjoyed playing with the other kids and eating his fill of the fresh homemade pies and cakes the other mothers brought.

At home at night, either his mom or dad would read a verse from the Bible aloud. His dad would caution Matt that to want material things was perfectly normal, but to be careful of the trap that worldly goods, if you let them, will come to possess you. Some folks, he explained, try to use material objects in order to fill the emptiness in their lives, but only God can bring us contentment and fulfillment. Before putting him to bed, Matt's parents always made sure he said his prayers and thanked God for all His blessings. When Matt and his family attended Mass on Sunday mornings, Father O'Mallory, the parish priest, spoke with his fiery Irish passion of God's hand and the many miracles He created. So Matt believed in the greatness of God and knew that somehow this day God had spoken to him and this moment was meant to be a preparation for something—for what, Matt didn't know. What he did know was that he had felt God's presence and gained a serenity far beyond his young years.

Mindlessly, still in a trancelike state, he slowly finished putting on his clothes, even pulling his jersey over his head as he suddenly felt the day lose its warmth, even though the sun was still in its midday position. It was a chill that would remain in his body throughout all his adult life.

He walked back to find his dad snoring on the bed of pine needles, exactly where he'd left him. He gently shook him awake and walked down to the water's edge to retrieve the trout they had caught, now in the wicker basket keeping cool in the shallow water. Normally a little chatterbox, Matt quietly packed up the fishing rods, picnic basket, and trash, leaving only their footprints in the dirt when they left. On the ride home, he thought it best not to share what had happened to him at the lake, and if his father sensed anything was amiss, he never mentioned it. Matt knew he'd experienced a miracle, just like the kind Father O'Mallory talked about in church that happened to everyday folk like him, but Matt needed to think on it for a while before speaking about it to anyone.

A sharp tug on his fishing line brought Matt's day-dreaming mind firmly back into the present. He could see a second trout had taken the bait and was trying to avoid his fate. The fish dived for the submerged log and was able to wrap the fishing line around a thick branch, snapping it. *Darn*, Matt thought. A great loneliness washed over him. He suddenly felt weak and lightheaded. His chest tightened into a steel band, and his breath became shallow, so he sat down against a large pine tree, putting his back and head against it. Somewhere off in the distance he could hear a coyote howl, echoing through the trees and off the mountainside. Matt peered down into the lake and watched a stream of bubbles rise to the surface, then break apart, each bubble reminiscent of his fleeting memories, not all pleasant, some cutting deep and painfully.

Matt and his family had lived in Millinocket, which to the summer folk was the jumping-off point to get to Baxter State Park, with its unspoiled beauty and remote wilderness. It offered unparalleled fishing, hunting, camping, hiking, canoeing, and of course the bane of every outdoorsman, thick swarms of black flies and mosquitoes. Most of the tourists—or "flatlanders," as his father would call them—cleared out long before the first snow fell, which could come as early as October, and then only the hardy residents would remain.

His parents told him that they had lived in Portland before he was born. By Maine standards, Portland was a big city. When Matt's mom became pregnant, they agreed not to raise their child there, with its ever-increasing pollution and crime. It was an easy decision to move upcountry, where they were from originally. Matt's father worked as a CPA in a large firm, but having been raised on a farm himself, he wanted to raise his child in the country, with the sweet smell in the air and the clear, cold, running streams. Where people still knew one another by their first names and cared about their neighbors. When the moon rose in the sky, the stars shined brightly, not having to compete with the big city lights. They sold their house to a couple from Boston, who thought moving to Portland was living in the country. With the proceeds of the sale, his mom and dad bought a forty-acre farm in Millinocket, and had enough money left over to buy a new John Deere tractor. There they raised some chickens and rabbits, had a dairy cow that provided milk that was not only fresh but also had the layer of sweet cream on the top, and made delicious homemade ice cream during the sizzling dog-days of August. They plowed twenty acres and planted rows of corn that was grown organically and thus fetched a pretty price from the people who were concerned with all the chemicals and pesticides now being used so liberally. The husks from the corn went to help feed the cow and the horse they had bought when Matt was born. Nothing went to waste. They believed God provided, but to waste was sinful. Matt's dad hunted, and every year, in addition to the ducks and rabbits he shot, he would put a deer in the freezer. Entertainment was usually the three of them, Matt and his parents, meeting at the small pond on the property at the end of a day's work, where Matt's mom would bring a pitcher of ice-cold, fresh-squeezed lemonade and a batch of homemade cookies. Matt was partial to the peanut butter ones his mom made that still had the impressions of the tines of the fork used to flatten the dough before baking. Before the lemonade was poured or a bite of cookie taken, Matt's mom or dad would say a quick prayer and thank God for all the blessings bestowed upon them, as well as for the world around them that gave them sustenance and such boundless beauty.

On Sundays mornings they attended Mass at the local Catholic Church, a weekly event for which almost the whole town turned out. They read the Bible, sang hymns, and heard the Word of the Lord from Father O'Mallory, a large, boisterous red-headed priest with an infectious laugh, who hailed from Ireland. After Mass, they would funnel down into the church basement to socialize over coffee and delicious dessert, depending on whose turn it was to provide the refreshment, and join in a raucous discussion of both the sermon and the local gossip and news in their small town. It was a weekly event that solidified them as a community. Father O'Mallory would listen to all their concerns and try to provide some insight into the teachings of the Bible, or even swap recipes with the ladies. As he watched his parishioners debate, he felt at home with these people, which was essential for him since he had no remaining living relatives and had not been born in this country. These were God-fearing people. Good people with loving and generous hearts.

Matt remembered back to the spring of 1985, when his dad had suffered a massive, fatal heart attack while on his John Deere tractor plowing the lower corn fields that ran along the creek bed. It was Matt who noticed the tractor moving erratically, with his dad slumped over the wheel, and screamed to his mother for help. She ran down from the front porch where she was reading the latest novel by

Stephen King, enjoying the warmth of the morning sun after a particularly long, sunless winter. She reached in and shut off the tractor's engine and yelled for Matt to run to the kitchen and call 911. By the time he reached it, he could barely see the numbers on the phone through the tears stinging his eyes and streaming down his face. He dialed the number and begged the dispatch operator to please hurry. Then, not knowing what else to do, he sat down on the yellow linoleum kitchen floor that his dad put in that winter. He remembered his mom said the old wooden floors were too dark and she wanted something bright and cheery. While Matt's dad liked the old hard pine floors better, with their grooves and hand-cut nails, he knew the kitchen was his wife's domain, so he readily agreed. Besides, he couldn't deny his wife anything. Ever since he'd met her at the high school barn dance just miles from where they lived now, he was smitten. She was the prettiest girl he had ever laid eyes on.

By the time the ambulance came, Matt's mom had taken her husband down off the tractor and was holding his head in her lap. She wept quietly as she lovingly stroked his hair. The paramedics checked his vitals and it was obvious he had passed, but they still had to wait until she finally was ready to release her husband from her arms some moments later, knowing she was holding him for the very last time.

The wake was held two days later at the local funeral home, the only funeral parlor in town. It was so small the townspeople joked about what would happen if two people died at the same time. Howard, the funeral director, was a stately, somber gentleman, perfectly suited for his profession, born in this very town many years past. When Matt's mom came in to make arrangements, he showed her to an aged Windsor chair that was stained with the memories and tears of the many grieving people who came before her. He offered her a cup of tea, which she gratefully accepted. Producing a thick leather binder, they went over the various prices of the services offered, the different styles and costs of the caskets, and where her husband would be finally laid to rest.

She chose a simple hard pine wooden casket with a white satin lining and a solitary cross carved on the top. She believed it was the one that best reflected both his life and simple servitude to God. There would not be any expense of flowers, as a dozen or more beautiful bouquets already had arrived. While she did appreciate those, she asked Howard to tell anyone who asked further about sending flowers to please make a donation to the poor box instead.

She buried her husband in the family plot in the town cemetery, which he had wisely bought for them when they first moved to town. They had already purchased the headstones for each other. All the necessary information— their names, dates of birth—was carved into the blackish grey granite that came from a quarry in Vermont. All that was missing was the date of death. They had chosen very simple stones with an engraved angel at the top looking down peacefully. When Matt was born, a superstitious bone emerged within his father, and he wouldn't buy his son a headstone, as if by doing so he'd somehow hasten his death. She had known this day would come, but had just not expected it so soon. Her husband always told her that death was inevitable, and that we should always be prepared for that day. He believed with all his heart, as did she, that only your earthly body dies, thus freeing your eternal soul. This should have provided her some small measure of comfort, but it didn't.

All the while his mother was making the arrangements, Matt sat solemnly by her side. No matter how hard he tried not to cry, a tear would appear and streak down his cheek. He would wipe it away with a closed fist and paw at his eyes. He tried to pay attention, thought it was important to do so, but was completely distracted by a series of flashbacks of his dad fishing, laughing, on his tractor, and quietly reading the Bible at night in his favorite chair by the fireplace.

At the wake, on both nights, Father O'Mallory was there for every minute, and paid particularly close attention to Matt, who had grown silent. While the townspeople and friends paid their last respects and signed the bound leather attendance book that lay open next to a crystal vase of lilies, Father O'Mallory sat beside Matt and told him that his father was a good and decent man, and he had no doubt whatsoever that he was now in heaven basking in God's love. Normally in a case like this, he knew a child this age would be angry at God, at the injustice of it all, which was perfectly normal and to be expected, but Matt accepted it with a grace normally reserved for much older people who had more experience with death. He looked up into Father O'Mallory's eyes and said that he was determined to obey God's task. The Father had no idea to what Matt was referring, but he let it go without further question.

Before he took over the parish in Millinocket, Father O'Mallory was the priest in an old stone church in Manhattan. His parishioners were almost all wealthy, some obscenely so, and drove to church in Mercedes Benzes, Jaguars, and Porsches. The men wore their finest gold watches and Armani suits, the women their designer clothes. They dressed for each other, not for God. Some he recognized as giants on Wall Street who were recipients of million-dollar bonuses, despite having invested some clients' life savings in risky stocks that resulted in their financial ruin. Others, prominent defense attorneys who made exorbitant fees representing organized crime figures. They listened halfheartedly to his sermon, more interested in seeing and being seen. The kingdom of heaven for them was an abstract concept, one that could be dealt with later, if at all. Their kingdom was here on Earth, and their God was power and money. They reminded him of the biblical parable about it being easier for a camel to pass through the eye of a needle than for a rich man to enter the kingdom of heaven.

When he heard of a small parish that was open in northern Maine, he asked for an immediate transfer, much to the surprise and disbelief of his own archdiocese. After completing the transfer paperwork, he was granted his request. He had been raised on a small sheep farm in County Cork, Ireland, the son of two pious but uneducated parents, and he knew he was going home where he truly belonged.

His new parishioners listened to his every word. God was a central part of their lives, not something thought about only on Sundays. They celebrated births, deaths, and everything in between in the small wood-framed building with the simple hard pine wooden pews they called their church. There were no gilded chalices or marble statues of saints, yet the humble families that came to Mass were unmatched in their devotion to God. When a winter storm blew down the steeple, splintering it into small pieces on the ground, the men of the area joined in and built another one while the women held a bake sale to raise the money for the necessary lumber and materials. In the summer the congregation would apply a fresh coat of white paint, and plant vibrant native wildflowers in the front. In the winter the men and boys would take turns helping Father O'Mallory clean the walk of snow and spread salt and ash on the walkway leading into the church to ensure no one would slip and fall. Whenever a parishioner was sick, neighbors would visit, bringing homemade food, and more importantly, the message that they cared.

After the funeral Mass on Sunday, Matt's house swelled with friends bringing covered casseroles, cakes and pastries, hams and roasts, and more food than they could ever eat. Most of it went into the freezer. The men offered their help if anything needed to be done on the farm, and the women offered to drop in daily to help out as well. His mother thanked them all, but graciously declined. She knew the sooner she got back to their *new* normal life, the better it would be for not only Matt, but for her as well.

The summer came and went. Matt fished and picked baskets of blackberries, blueberries, and strawberries that grew wild on their farm. His mother noted with sadness that he no longer swung on the rope that his father put on the old oak tree down by the creek, or tossed the basketball at the rim attached to the barn door. He rarely went out with his friends, instead preferring to stay on the farm with her. Even when he went fishing, it was more to put food in the freezer than when he had done it just for fun and excitement. He placed his fishing pole in the mudroom attached to the house, still next to his dad's. When she suggested he use his father's rod, which was of a better size for him now that he had grown, he just shook his head no. His dad had given him his, and, well, he just couldn't get around to giving it up. Not yet. She knew he was taking the death hard—she was, too—but she just couldn't replace her husband's role in raising a young boy. Time heals all, she prayed.

She baked pies for herself and Matt, always baking an extra couple to give to their neighbors to repay them for their kindness. Growing up on a farm herself, she had no trouble finishing the planting and numerous chores that a working farm requires. She was not afraid of hard work since her father had given her an equal share of the chores when she was a child. She knew how to run a tractor as well as any man. Her dad had an old red Ford tractor that looked like it should be in an antique show. He'd laugh and say you were paying for the green paint when you bought a Deere. He taught her how to run it and how to fix it if it broke. Girls were as important as boys when it came to chores on a farm, he loved to say.

Matt, now eleven, helped out after school, feeding the animals, putting up hay, and hunting up small game to put meat on the table. When her husband was alive, Matt's mother couldn't remember the last time they bought beef. They both knew that game was leaner and healthier to eat. Besides, didn't God put them on His Earth to provide? But come the fall, she figured that for the first time in years, she might have to buy half a steer to put in the freezer, as she was sure to run out of venison. So it was a wonderful surprise when one Sunday after Mass, Father O'Mallory offered to take Matt deer hunting.

"Father, you know how to hunt?" she said with surprise.

"Ah, my good woman, who do you think put fresh meat on my father's table when I was growing up in Ireland, and what do you think I eat now?" he said with a loud laugh, his hands on his ample girth.

So late that fall, Matt and Father O'Mallory took to the woods. On opening day, he picked Matt up at his farm at three in the morning, long before the first light graced the fields, and even earlier than the old bantam rooster began to crow. Matt remembered asking his dad why the rooster crowed so early in the morning. His dad used to kid and say that it was the only time the old rooster could get a word in edgewise living with all those hens.

Father O'Mallory drove an old green four-wheel drive Subaru that had both a Bible and a gun in the back. He always said you never knew when you'd need either one of them. Matt and his mom were waiting for him on the front porch before daybreak, and although she invited him in for a hunter's breakfast and coffee, she knew they wanted to get an early start. She gave Matt two thermoses filled with steaming hot coffee to take with them. One thermos filled with black for Father, one with milk and sugar for Matt. Along with the coffee came four thick chicken salad sandwiches, fruit, and a handful of grain bars. She used to hunt herself and knew the effort expended traipsing through the woods and the growling stomachs that followed right behind.

They loaded up the car and headed out to the woods. All in all it was a dull, drab day. The sky was overcast with dark clouds, and a cold, wet wind blew down off Mt. Katahdin. Matt guided Father O'Mallory to the same spot where he had gone so many times with his dad. It had been some time since he'd had his vision, and he didn't know how he felt about going back to the same vicinity, but the feeling of love he had for his dad, and the curiosity of going back to the site of his own miracle, pushed him forward.

The familiar dirt road that led to the hunting spot wound its way over an uneven hill filled with deep ruts and fallen branches. They drove by the cutoff the first time without seeing it, nature having closed its opening with disuse. Doubling back, Matt pointed it out, and Father O'Mallory pulled up to it. They had to take a small axe and camp saw to cut away the gnarled stumps and overgrown branches that blocked their path. It was still dark, and the cold northern wind of the forest whipped up, tugging at their jackets.

With a short drive through the trees, they had no trouble finding an opening to park their car. Both got out silently, quietly closing the car doors, knowing how both the sounds and the smell of their presence carried deep into the woods and would spook the deer. Although previously having agreed to hunt together, Matt said that his father allowed him to hunt by himself, but within yelling range of one another. Father O'Mallory said he couldn't do that just yet. The Father had brought two stainless steel whistles attached to a strip of brown rawhide to hang around their necks in the event they did get separated and could not hear one another. Both were excellent hunters, careful of gun safety, and mindful of the enormous responsibility of aiming and shooting a high powered rifle, unlike some of the city folk that come to the Maine woods to hunt but inevitably, every hunting season, would shoot some other hunter.

They loaded their guns in silence. Matt had an older lever action Winchester .30-30 that his dad had bought used for him from the neighbor down the road. It had a crack in the stock, but it shot straight. Father O'Mallory had a Ruger bolt action .30-06, a gift from his parishioners on his first Christmas. After checking to make sure they had their maps designating exactly the area they would be hunting in, checking their compasses, synchronizing their watches, loading their backpacks with food and raincoats, and agreeing on a time to meet back at the car should they lose sight of one another, they headed out down a small trail that circled the lake. Matt led the hunt, carefully and silently picking his way, his feet lightly touching the ground, avoiding stepping on any branch that might crack and alert the deer of their presence. He moved slowly, taking one step and then waiting a moment before taking the next, just like his father taught him. The going was slow as the trail led up a ravine to a bluff that overlooked the lake below. He turned often at first to make sure the Father was behind him since there was a notable absence of noise coming from his rear. He was amazed the big man could move so quietly, and by the grin on the Father's face, he must have read Matt's mind.

Matt walked for a while before he stopped to admire the early morning sun breaking out over the horizon and gleaming off the lake. He thought of his dad. His father always told him that there were so many precious moments given to us by God that we just walked by, in too much of a hurry to see the beauty that unfurled before us. It started to rain again, just a few drops, but enough to wet their faces and chill their bodies. The treetops were now beginning to appear in the mist rolling off the mountain.

Matt picked up a movement to his left, coming from a blown-down alder. A large buck, seemingly still unaware of the presence of the man and the boy, moved effortlessly through the native brush and branches with a fluid, soundless motion. Matt waited for the buck to drop his head to browse, and when he did, Matt raised his gun and fired the killing shot. He stopped and paused for a moment before he walked over to the deer, now lying motionless on the ground. Father O'Mallory walked up beside him. There were no high-fives or back slapping, celebrating the kill. Instead, the Father put his hand on Matt's shoulder and said, "We must give thanks." Matt went to his knees, and both bowed their heads.

"Heavenly Father, we give thanks for giving us life and for the countless blessings You have bestowed upon us. Thank You for this gift of meat to sustain us, for the water that slakes our thirst, and for Your love that surrounds us. Amen."

"Amen," Matt replied. He pulled at Father O'Mallory's coat sleeve and motioned with his head across the lake toward Mt. Katahdin. The cirrus clouds that had previously covered the mountains in a white shroud parted, just for a moment, revealing the beauty of the peak towering majestically into the sky. Looking at the vista, the Father and Matt felt the humility God teaches us through His grand design in nature, with its intricate patterns and peaceful orderliness.

Matt pulled out his hunting knife and went to work cleaning his deer. He carefully removed the inside organs, placing the heart and liver in separate plastic bags. The hide, tawny brown, thick and luxurious, would be salted and stretched on the side of the barn. It would fetch a handsome price from the tannery for people in the city wanting deerskin gloves. Everything that could be used would be used. Nothing would go to waste. The Father watched Matt work, impressed by the young man's skill and reverence. When he was finished cleaning the buck, he attached a thick white nylon rope around its horns to pull it back to camp. Father O'Mallory wanted to help, but it was mostly downhill, and Matt wanted to do it by himself. The Father relieved him of his rifle and backpack, and the pair, one man and one boy, slowly walked back down the ravine. The rain changed into a driving sleet, then snow, which began to accumulate rapidly. By the time they reached the car, a blanket of pure white covered the silent forest floor.

That day forged a close relationship. Father O'Mallory became a father figure and surrogate for Matt. They hunted and fished together often, and the Father tutored Matt in Bible studies. Matt was so interested that one day he told Father O'Mallory he was going to join the priesthood.

Matt snapped out of his daydreaming when the movement of a coyote caught his eye crossing the trail in front of him, unhurried and unmolested.

The sun had just begun to dip below the mountain and cast a long, wide shadow across the lake. Matt felt a shudder and pulled his sweater tightly around him. He had better be getting back to camp.

How did we get to this point? How could this have happened to America? He became overwhelmed and felt very, very old. He knew the rest of his *family*—at least that's what they called themselves—depended on him to lead. He delegated as much as possible, but they looked to him for answers that he did not have, or for comfort he could not give. He watched a leaf fall down in the stream, tossed helplessly about with the current. He could readily identify with it.

He pulled himself up, dusting the dirt off his faded and torn jeans, carrying his lone fish, and headed back to camp. The younger members had been pushing for violent action against the Chinese, still itching to avenge the killing at the church. Matt promised to address them tonight over dinner.

Winter 2028

WHITE HOUSE

A T MIDDAY, Xi Chang looked out onto the expansive rolling lawn of the White House. It was covered with a thin, translucent blanket of snow and frosted with tiny icicles that sparkled like scattered diamonds. He stood on the second-story balcony and ran his hands along the pitted white granite railing, and thought of how many American presidents had done the same before him. Behind him was the Executive Office Building, or more commonly known to the public as the West Wing. This was Xi's command center. It was from here that he launched his worldwide military strategic plan. He smiled. The first cornerstone of the White House was laid by the famous American general and first president of the United States, George Washington. The White House and its occupants had represented the epicenter of American imperialism, greed, arrogance, corruption, and world power for more than two hundred years. That period of glory was all over now. America was crushed, and the Chinese red flag of five stars replaced the Stars and Stripes.

Xi reflected pensively upon the United States' unconditional surrender to his regime. Following the surrender, he summarily ordered the destruction of all monuments and symbols of American power. He was not going to give any false hope to the Americans, or let them think they could create a separate sovereign nation as they had foolishly allowed the Native Americans to do.

First he bulldozed the dome-shaped rotunda of the Jefferson Memorial, leaving the rubble heaped in a pile for all to see. Next he destroyed the Washington Monument, the Lincoln Memorial, and the Iwo Jima Memorial, which represented American military prowess and imperialism. At the Arlington National Cemetery, the bulldozers swept away the gravestones of John F. Kennedy and the Tomb of the Unknown Soldier alike, leaving just a barren, scarred field in their place. He took down the American flag that flew over the White House and threw it on top of the burning pile of their *priceless* historical documents and memorabilia that had previously adorned the walls of the Capitol. As a final gesture, although he did appreciate their beauty, he cut down the 3,750 Yoshino cherry blossom trees that the Japanese sent to America in 1912 as a token of their friendship. It was not lost on Xi that these "friends" then launched the infamous sneak attack on Pearl Harbor that catapulted the United States into the war. Friends, thought Xi, were a luxury he did not seek or require.

Xi's native tongue was Mandarin, but he also spoke fluent English and Spanish. He excelled as a student of history and knew that the best way to control a conquered people was to harshly abolish any ray of hope they might possess. Hope nurtured rebellion.

As the sun's rays glistened through the ice that formed on the upper branches of the pine trees, he mused on how far he had come and what a different world he now lived in. He lifted his face to the sky and let the sun shine on him. The warmth filled him with a deep satisfaction. Below, there were sounds of a flurry of activity. He could smell the pungent odor of diesel fuel from the convoy of military jeeps and troop transport trucks, with their red star displayed on their doors, surrounding the White House, turning the previously manicured lawns into wide strips of muddy dirt. He could hear the bark of his military commanders issuing orders to their troops. The commands were punctuated by the shrill screams of the captured Americans. The prisoners were restrained by heavy, rough iron shackles that bit cruelly into their naked arms and legs, as they awaited execution. Public executions sowed fear into onlookers, and demonstrated that even minimal dissension would not be tolerated. The punishment for all infractions was the same: death by firing squad.

The more vocal rebels were crucified. Although crucifying prisoners was time consuming and not very practical to do on a large scale, he knew it had a devastating effect on the crowds who were forced to watch. When they were dragged to the large wooden crosses, some called out for Jesus, but most just cried and pleaded for the pain to stop. Low-pitched sobbing emanated from the gallery of onlookers as his men drove large sharpened iron spikes into the hands and feet of the prisoners. The guards were men specially chosen for their penchant for cruelty. They would taunt the Americans by asking them why their God didn't save them, and saying that they should be happy they were being crucified as their savior Jesus had been.

At age sixty-eight, Xi was the Paramount Leader of China, which was to say he was the supreme and sole political authority in charge of the three biggest government sectors China had: the State, the Media, and the Military. His other official titles were General Secretary of the Communist Party, Chairman of the Central Committee, and Chairman of the Central Military Commission. China's official name was the People's Republic of China, but it was never confused with being a government of the people. Xi Chang solely ruled with a draconian hand and tolerated no dissent. Dissidents either ended up in Siberia and were worked to death, or were simply summarily brought into a courtyard and shot. He took no counsel other than his own.

In 1960, Xi was born into a poor rural farming family, scratching out a hardscrabble existence on a small plot of rocky soil they leased in the rice terraced mountains of Yunnan. At that time, farmers were not allowed to own land but instead were part of the People's Commune System. Each farmer would have about a half-acre plot of land in which to grow their crops. The lucky ones might have a pig or a chicken or two, but most were able to grow only enough to feed their families, with little left over to sell at market. Others, not as fortunate, starved.

Xi's family lived in a small one-room hut his father had built using scraps of wood he salvaged in the country-side. There was a small outhouse behind, and his mother cooked their simple meals of rice and slivers of fish, when they could trade for it, over an open hearth with charcoal. The family wore simple cotton pants and shirts they would wash in the nearby stream, with thin leather sandals for their feet. Xi's father and mother worked in the fields all day, planting by hand the green shoots of rice, sometimes not even returning to their home until nightfall. Farming was incessant, backbreaking work and complicated by the severe shortage of arable land. The difference between having a successful crop or not could be life itself.

When Xi was barely a toddler, the family crops were destroyed by locusts. A full season of hard work was gone in one frenzied feeding flash. Growing barely enough potatoes and rice to survive, and not being able to afford feeding another hungry mouth, his father went to the local village head for help. Xi's father was told of a man in the military who was looking to adopt a son, as his wife could not bear children. He would pay good money for a healthy boy. Xi's mother cried and pleaded with her husband not to sell their only child, but her pleas fell on deaf ears. Later that week, he took Xi to the village. The soldier, who was actually a captain in the Chinese army, picked up and inspected the baby. Satisfied it was healthy, he offered Xi's father a year's wages, which amounted to one hundred and twenty US dollars, and a water buffalo, which would help him in the fields. Xi's father accepted the offer and handed his son over to the captain, sadly knowing he would never see him again. He did not.

Xi never knew his parents or whether or not he had any siblings. He tried to remember them, but the memories had faded. Sometimes a random image would just pop into his head, but he didn't know if it was real or just a fabrication of his young mind yearning to recall. When he was nine years old, his adoptive father told him without emotion that his parents had drowned in a flash flood. With this information, Xi shut the door on his past. His adoptive mother became ill and died shortly after his tenth birthday. The loss of the only mother he had known left him bereft. He often cried himself to sleep, careful not to let his father hear his quiet sobs. While his father provided his basic needs, he was far from nurturing, and would view Xi's tears as a sign of weakness.

Oftentimes, Xi's father would leave on covert military missions that were neither discussed nor explained to the small boy. Xi was left in the hands of the housekeeper and her husband, who did the cooking and cleaning for the family. They had no children of their own and relished spending time alone with him. The husband would eke out time from his duties to play with the young boy, and his wife would make special sesame rice balls that he loved. Since Xi's father had forbidden the housekeepers from spoiling the child, they were careful to keep their affections clandestine.

Xi had very little social interaction with other children and thus became a loner who buried himself in the many history and military books that his father had collected. He especially liked the teaching of the famous Chinese General Sun Tzu, who wrote the extremely influential book on military strategy *The Art of War*. He also favored the historical accounts of the Mongolian warlord Genghis Khan. Those early readings would help shape the man he would become.

When Xi turned eleven, he attended the Central Party School, which was the ideological heart of the Communist Party. He excelled in mathematics and science, and studied Uechi-ryu, an ancient Okinawan form of self-defense. His exemplary academic performance caught the attention of the military leaders who ran the school. Much to his delight, Xi was selected for further advancement. During this time a singular event occurred that would shape his life forever.

As a Chinese citizen, Xi was aware of the long historical pattern of mutual suspicion and hostility between China and Russia. It was similar to the manner in which American children knew about the conflict between their fledgling country and England's domination that led to the Revolutionary War. Chinese students were taught that from 1949 to 1958, Russia made military incursions in the area of Northwest Xinjiang, seizing by force almost three million square kilometers of Chinese land. This conquest was used to teach the young students to always regard the Russians with suspicion and mistrust.

In 1968, Russia invaded Czechoslovakia in order to seize more land. While the USSR never admitted that acquisition of more territory was its goal, that action gave rise to suspicions by the Chinese about Russia's intentions toward them. Sharp border clashes began to occur along the Ussuri River, and tension heightened between the two powerful nations.

In 1971, when Xi was eleven, the Chinese, fearing a Soviet strike into China on their nuclear testing facilities in Xinjiang, sent his father on a secret mission into Russia with a handful of trained operatives to assess the Russian military strength in the area. It was a highly classified operation and only involved Xi's father and three other trained military commandos. Unbeknownst to the group, one of the men was an agent working for the Russians. The men were captured, given a mock trial, and executed. Their bodies were never recovered. What was particularly painful for Xi was that the man who betrayed the group was his father's best friend, and was like an uncle to Xi. A man who had shared many meals at his home and had bounced Xi on his knee when he was a young child. His hatred for the Russians and his fealty to China cemented. He also learned to trust no one but himself, a lesson he would carry with him into his adult life.

Upon graduating the Central Party School, he joined the People's Liberation Army, or PLA. After two years of training, he quickly advanced to the rank of sergeant. He was stationed at a remote outpost near Lake Balkhash on the border between Russia and China, a site of past conflicts. One dark, moonless night, while on patrol he spied a column of camouflaged Russian soldiers silently crossing into Chinese territory. A firefight ensued, but his squad was overrun and half of his men were killed, including his company commander. He rallied the remaining troops and counter attacked. Against the standing orders at that time, Xi pursued them back into Russian territory and captured them. With his squad leader dead, Xi assumed command. He refused to take any captives. The thought of his father being betrayed and then executed had forever hardened his heart. He walked up to each Russian, now bound and kneeling, coldly pointed his pistol, and fired a bullet one by one into their heads, letting them fall lifelessly onto the blood-soaked ground. His fellow soldiers would whisper how he insisted on personally executing the Russians, no matter how much the captives cried or begged for their lives. When Chinese troops arrived to relieve them, Xi was sent to Zhongnanhai, the massive government building in the capital of Beijing, to give a full account of his actions. He fully expected to be severely disciplined, if not executed himself. The Chinese did not favor individual thoughts or actions, and he had disobeyed a direct standing order not to enter Russian territory, let alone taking it upon himself to execute prisoners who had surrendered, offering no further threat.

Xi reported for his disciplinary hearing dressed in his khaki green military uniform, freshly starched and pressed. He stood at attention and reported to the tribunal the facts of the skirmish as they occurred. The captured Russians had violated Chinese territory, as they had many times, and the ensuing firefight resulted in the death of his commanding officer and half the men of his squad. He believed the Chinese military should not tolerate that kind of aggression. The policy was to deal with such attacks severely in order to send an emphatic message that China would not tolerate outside interference in its affairs. Xi explained that he executed the Russian captives because they were enemies of the State. He testified to the committee that he alone fired on the Russians, and the responsibility for their deaths rested solely on his shoulders. His fellow comrades should not be punished for his actions.

The committee listened dispassionately to Xi's account. At the conclusion of his testimony, they took a brief recess to discuss the matters in chambers. Xi stood motionless awaiting his fate. The committee returned to the hearing room and advised him that they needed additional time to make a decision since the ruling had not been unanimous. He was dismissed and told he would be notified of their decision. For an agonizing long time Xi wondered if he would suffer the same fate as his father, only this time at the hands of his own country, for his disobedience. Three days later he was summoned to meet with the committee and told he was being promoted to the rank of captain and appointed to the Central Military Commission as part of a special new division, the Black Tigers, or 黑老虎, dealing in covert operations. He would answer only to them. Until now Xi had been expecting the worst, so he received the promotion in stunned silence, thanked the committee, and left to assume his new duties.

He quickly rose through the ranks of the Black Tigers, demonstrating a brilliant mind for military strategy and a ruthless willingness to carry out whatever the mission required. By the time he was thirty, he was the sole leader of the operation, and was granted unprecedented latitude in planning and executing operations. Such singular decision making was unheard of at that time. In 2013, at the young age of fifty three, Xi was asked to become one of only seven members of China's Standing Committee, a select group that dealt in affairs that went beyond China's borders and governed the other ruling factions.

Previously, in 2011, China was faced with a population explosion of 1.3 trillion people, compounded by a high birth rate of 12.29 per 1,000, while life expectancy climbed to 74.68 years; China was running out of natural resources, especially land. Although stewards of 3,600 million square miles, most was too mountainous, and the Gobi desert to the north was unfit to homestead. Eight hundred million rural peasants lived on the equivalent of less than three hundred US dollars annually. Considering at the time the world's population was 6.7 trillion, 20 percent of the world's citizens were Chinese; a staggering one in five. To further complicate matters, China's close ally North Korea was in a never-ending famine, with millions dying of starvation. More ominous, China had a hostile Russia on its border.

Something had to be done.

In 2015, Xi put forth a white paper to his committee proposing that China begin to aggressively export some of its more technically trained people to other countries, especially students in good standing with the Chinese Communist Party. This would serve two purposes: It would open up avenues in the future for more Chinese to inhabit foreign territory; and second, and more nefarious, it would set up a base of operations for espionage and infiltration. His suggestion was unanimously accepted, and Xi was elected as chairman of the Standing Committee.

At the time, China had a robust economy, with a national debt of only 15.6 percent of its GNP, or roughly 2.2 trillion yuan, the national currency. This was mainly due to the fact that most European countries and America took advantage of the cheap Chinese labor—relaxed environmental and human rights conditions. These countries built factories in China in which to manufacture their designer goods to be shipped back home. All of this accounted for the Chinese having a large surplus of hard currency.

That year China invested millions of dollars in Cuba, building a state-of-the-art technological center, and with it thousands of Chinese to staff it and implement a training program for the Cubans. The Cuban economy, having suffered through an ill-advised boycott by the United States and the subsequent loss of Russia's financial aid, eagerly accepted the trade. With eleven million Cubans inhabiting this island just seventy miles south of the US shores, the influx of Chinese was barely noticed by the American government, and was not deemed a threat.

China took this model and expanded it. Most countries welcomed the Chinese money and the technology that came with it. So the Chinese infiltrated the Bahamas, Argentina, Venezuela, Central America, Africa, and what would be the most devastating in years to come for the United States, Mexico.

The *Red Terror* had begun.

Five years later, in 2020, China was faced with a devastating drought that lasted for three years. The drought dried up the rivers and decimated the rice crops. Mass starvation began to occur in rural areas, and China was pushed to the brink. They sought help in purchasing grains, especially wheat from the United States and Canada, but had a shortfall of hard currency due to the unwise policies of the previous Central Committee that lent the United States over 17 trillion dollars. China approached the United States to arrange terms to purchase the grains necessary to feed their people, and was shocked to learn that for all practical purposes, the United States could not pay back but a small portion of the trillions borrowed. Worse still was that the president of the United States, Richard P. Mann, recognizing a way to exploit the Chinese famine and decrease the amount of debt owed to them, said that the United States would sell China 500,000 metric tons of both wheat and corn, but at 400 percent above the world commodity's going rate. China, as well as the rest of the world, was shocked by this action but could do nothing; their people were starving in the streets. So the Paramount Leader Li Wanquan reluctantly accepted the deal.

The acceptance of this deal sent shock waves through the Central Committee. Xi Chang was neither shocked nor angry. Xi had little respect for America, nor was he surprised when they held a gun to China's head. The United States used her military might to interfere in other nations' governments, and preached moral responsibility and conservation yet consumed almost half of the world's natural resources. It forbade other nations to develop nuclear weapons yet had an arsenal of its own that could destroy the world many times over. He knew that China would never be accepted as an equal by the United States, Canada, Britain, or the rest of the Western world. China would always be viewed as a vassal unless something drastic was done. Xi knew that the average American stereotyped a Chinese citizen as a maker of trinkets or fireworks, or a purveyor of take-out food.

That would change.

In 2022, as the chairman of the Central Military Commission and the ranking member of the Standing

Committee, Xi led a military coup and took sole command over the People's Republic of China. The People's Liberation Army, sickened by the weakness of their political leaders and their hatred of America, rallied around the nationalism Chang espoused.

Chang wasted no time in arresting the ruling party, and in one bold move charged them with treason against the People's Republic of China, sentencing them to death. They were dragged out into the main square in front of a howling bloodthirsty crowd, and to the sounds of jeering, were executed by firing squad.

The war with the United States began to formalize in Xi's mind.

Winter 2028

WASHINGTON DC

XI LEFT THE balcony and entered the White House Situation Room. He had summoned his team of advisors for the early-morning strategy session, and they were already waiting for him. Although he made all his decisions independently, he did respect what the members of his team had to say; however, he never ruled by consensus. He walked over to the wall where various maps of the world were hung, his eyes taking in the numbers and red arrows marking the location of the deployed Chinese military troops. On his desk an ornate white opaque ivory carved bust of Genghis Khan that had once sat on his father's desk was now surrounded by military position papers and graphs indicating current troop strength and Chinese causalities; the numbers of the dead foreigners meant very little to him. With this information he decided future pending military actions.

He poured a steaming hot cup of tea from a centuries-old porcelain pot. It was inlayed with red dragons over a green background surrounded by a delicate gold border, brought from China to America. Raising the hot liquid to his lips, he began to address his men.

"Comrades, China is on the verge of fulfilling its true destiny as the sole world leader. We are an ancient civilization, the first *civilized* nation. The T'ang dynasty brought the world painting, sculpture, and poetry; the invention of wood block printing, which allowed the first mass production of books, and thus education for the masses. Yet our nation was brought to its knees time and time again by invading foreign interests. Our religion made us weak. It practiced peace and enlightenment, yet when our enemies brought death and rape to our doors, it had no answers other than to pray and meditate! Still, our leaders, woefully mistaken and weak, sought peaceful solutions. We opened up our markets to the Americans, and they became our largest trading partner. When America needed to borrow trillions to sustain its wasteful capitalistic government, our leaders lent it to them. *Trillions* to a country with no moral spine!"

Xi paused and took a sip of his tea, his face impassive as he gazed at his people.

"When our own economy began to slow down in 2020 and we suffered a devastating drought, we *requested* a partial amount of our money be returned to us. Our own cash flow had decreased with the global recession, and we were getting to a point where scarce funds inhibited our ability to purchase wheat, corn, oil, and other commodities on the world market sorely needed to sustain our people. *Over 17 trillion they owed us! Our money! Money we had lent them so their citizens could buy houses they could not afford, luxury cars, gold watches they did not need, jewelry to adorn themselves, luxury boats and vacations bought on credit, all on BORROWED money, while our farmers were forced to live on pennies a day! Money they GAVE to other countries that hated them! Iraq, Iran, Syria, Egypt! OUR MONEY! BORROWED FROM US! And what was the United States' response? They REFUSED US!*

They said they didn't have it! The most powerful nation on Earth was BROKE!"

Xi slammed his fist on the table.

"Our leaders failed its people, and that is what led to our overthrow of the weak Central Committee government by the People's Liberation Army. What the politicians failed to realize was that lending vast sums of money time and time again to the Americans was like lending money to a degenerate opium user. You must know, sooner or later, you will not get your money back.

"We had almost two *trillion* people facing starvation. *Two trillion!* In the countryside, people who were unable to get to the cities resorted to eating grass and bark to fill their stomachs while the Americans grew fat. So we took matters into our own hands. We realized that China was provided a historic opportunity to solve critical problems including our lack of living space and food for our people, as well as much-needed raw materials. We began to develop military plans to protect our ancient nation. While we negotiated with the US for grain, our scientists, the best in the world, developed new software for a prototype of computers accessible only to us. We knew the extent of the US spying on us and countered by developing a new satellite uplink system that would provide security and privacy in all communications. A power source hidden deep within our mountains supports this technology. Our engineers developed computer software that would not interface with the existing systems utilized by the rest of the world. Thus our military communications and war plans remained covert. We constructed our navy, especially the twenty nuclear-powered fast-attack submarines, each capable of launching sixteen intercontinental missiles tipped with nuclear explosives. As you are now aware, our most devastating weapon in the war with the US was the development of the most powerful NEMP, or nuclear electromagnetic pulse bomb. Now let us talk about the present."

Xi walked over to the wall and pointed to the United States. Red Chinese flags were over every major US city and population center. Every major airport was under Chinese control. Any small American plane that dared to attempt to fly anywhere to escape was identified by radar, tracked, and shot down. On every major highway Chinese checkpoints had been established. In addition, war ships and smaller armed boats patrolled the waterways.

He called on Wang Sheng Kun, his domestic advisor to the United States. "How many Americans are left alive?"

"Sir, when we attacked America three years ago, there was a population of a little over three hundred and fifty million. The majority, as you know, were living in populated cities on both coasts. I'm pleased to say with the implementation of our forced labor camps—and to a much lesser degree, our executions—the population now is estimated to be somewhere around one hundred and fifty million."

"Very good. Have you a targeted goal?"

"Yes. We require about 800,000 to 900,000 to keep as a slave labor force. No more than that. Our people have been taking over all the normal functions of the US. We now have about two million of our citizens relocated throughout the grain belt, and we're mastering all the variables of the farming operations here and in Canada. We of course anticipated the time needed to repair the damage done by our NEMP attacks, and that is also ahead of schedule.

"Our fishermen have repaired and subsequently commanded all the American super-trawlers operating on both coasts, and the harvest is already enough to feed our people."

"The remaining Americans...?" Xi asked.

"Still on starvation rations, as you stipulated. We allow them about eight hundred calories per person daily, which is just enough to keep them alive and able to labor. Most of their food comes from our scraps. None of the grains or fish we harvest is diverted to them for sustenance."

"No food riots or problems?"

"None, sir. Any man or woman—or child, for that matter—who causes a problem is publically executed, a consequence that deters rebellious activity. For the most part, the Americans are cowering in their homes."

"Excellent! In five years' time, the American population will be decimated. We'll have no further use for them. Very good. We need America. Not the Americans."

Turning back toward the map of the United States, Xi asked, "Now where do we stand on crushing the rebellion? Yang?"

Yang Keqiang, military advisor for the United States, answered, "Sir, the United States collapsed as you predicted. When we arrived, there were breakaway factions of the military which refused to surrender. Lack of communication between those factions, and lack of real leadership, enabled our troops to mop those up fairly easily. Again, sir, your edict proclaiming that to resist and refuse to turn in their weapons would result in the execution of families worked perfectly. The Americans, as we anticipated, had no stomach for rebellion once we began shooting their wives and children. As for the famed militia, they were scattered, unable to communicate with one another, allowing us to pick them off one by one. I must confess they fought valiantly, but again, they were just not formidable opponents for our crack troops."

"So we're in complete control?"

"Apart from a few roving hunter-kill squads left over from the military and some smaller militia outfits operating in the more remote areas of the country, yes, sir. We do have Apache helicopter gunships tracking and destroying some of them. It's just a matter of time before we eliminate them all. We are monitoring their transmissions via ham radios, and some other groups were content to slip away anonymously into the wilderness areas, but they pose no problems to our plans."

"I want them all destroyed. Our troops are to kill them on sight. Make an example of them. And what of my edict forbidding religion?"

"Interesting enough, sir, while it's true that America was founded on its Christian faith and a strong belief in God, over the centuries the people moved away from it on their own. The religious moral fiber of Christian values was weakened by their own unbridled selfishness and greed. America became a country of the very rich and the very poor. The wealthy had the best access to health care while the poor languished and died in the streets. Americans turned away from their God long before we took over, so enforcing the edict about worship and the destruction of their churches was a fairly simple task."

Chang responded, "Still, we must be vigilant about a resurgence. Karl Marx wisely said religion was the opium of the masses. Enforce the rule with brutal force. Anyone caught praying in a church we haven't destroyed yet is to be flogged until their skin peels off and then crucified...publically. I plan to stamp out religious worship globally. That was the first thing I did when I assumed power in China, and we need to make an example of the Americans to the rest of the world. When we take this *myth* of God away from them, they have nothing."

Pausing to command the full attention of his military leaders, Xi went on to say, "Our priority is singularly focused on controlling the world's resources and expanding the living area for our citizens. We now have complete control of all the resources in North America and Central America. Our position to the world is simple: join us, and live; resist, and be destroyed. For this we will emulate the great Genghis Khan. He too was driven to conquer for environmental reasons. As his people's food and resources became scarce, he did not *ask,* he took. He was a fearless warlord, piling the skulls of men, women, and children who opposed him in large pyramidal mounds. Khan attacked his enemies with unstoppable savagery. They would rather surrender than suffer his attacks, and that is exactly our military plan.

"We have the only viable economy remaining in the world. When we destroyed the dollar, the Euro and the Pound collapsed. Capitalistic countries that treated us as a third-world nation reverted to bartering as they did five hundred years ago. We have outlawed and replaced their currency with our yuan. The people of those nations no longer have weapons. We took those away. Apart from a small standing army, their populace relied on America to keep them safe. After we detonated a nuclear bomb over Scotland and another over Sri Lanka, any thoughts of military opposition ceased. We required all nations to accept the dismantling of their nuclear arsenal or risk immediate annihilation. We do allow them to maintain a small local defense for police purposes, under our jurisdiction of course, but all standing military had to be dismantled.

Now European countries may *think* of themselves as our trading partner, but they are ruled by China and tread lightly.

"Our simultaneous NEMP attack on Russia was also a complete success. Most of what they had in the way of nukes was dismantled in a joint peace treaty with the United States years ago. When we offered to share in North America's bounty with them, they knew it was better to become our vassal than oppose us. They do have a large standing army, but that too is being dismantled. Russia was compelled to allow us to share in their vast oil and coal reserves. We'll keep a close eye on the Russians, but I don't expect any problems. The savagery we showed upon the Americans was not lost on them."

Turning again to the map and pointing to Africa, Xi continued, "This whole continent is ours. They had no weapons or troop strength to oppose us. Our troops and leadership have in one quick year commanded every key position. Africa holds vast amounts of uranium, iron, and copper, in addition to coltan, the mineral China needs since it is critical to our computer processor's performance. With the new world economy, where the only currency is our yuan, they do have gold, but it is not as important as it once was, although it still has some uses in technology. Same for their diamonds. The advantage in controlling the world's economy is that we determine what a valuable currency is and what is not. By outlawing the trading or sale of gold and diamonds, we can fully control the economic marketplace.

"Australia will give us some coal, natural gas, and iron ore, but the prize is its rich deposits of uranium ore, which we can refine for our nuclear power. We will put off any invasion there until we've dealt with the other major global powers. We can expect resistance, necessitating a commitment of troops to both Australia and New Zealand. They are both countries that should know when they are defeated, but the Aussies and Kiwis love a good fight, no matter what the odds. The goal is not to utilize nuclear weapons. It will be implemented only as a last resort. We'll deal with them after we deal with the Middle East.

"North America was our greatest prize. Grains, natural gas and coal deposits, cattle, timber, and, of course, land. It has everything we need to expand and subsequently sustain our citizens. Mexico, not so much. Some agricultural growth and, of course, the native black bean, which is high in protein and ideal for exportation to North Korea as a food staple. Mexico had no viable government. It is ruled by warring drug cartels, and we have a working relationship with them at the moment. They are well aware they're not dealing with the weak-kneed politicians from Washington. The cartels may peddle their drugs if the drugs and the infighting is contained to Central America. If not, it has been made clear that we have no problem utilizing Chinese nukes. Mexico is not essential and is of little value."

"And what of Japan, sir?"

Xi turned quickly, his lips pulled back in a sneer. "Japan will cease to exist. We will wipe them off the map! Nanking will be finally avenged. China has a long memory when it comes to the atrocities Japan committed against us. Three hundred thousand innocent and unarmed men, women, and children murdered and raped at the hands of the cowardly Japanese army. I for one celebrated when the Americans bombed their cities. I have already informed North Korea that both South Korea and Japan are theirs to do with as they choose, providing it includes exterminating those vermin from the face of the Earth. Without the help of the US military, neither country can stand on its own. This should appease our friends in North Korea and solve their need for land and food. Killing the Japanese should satisfy their bloodlust."

Turning toward the Middle East he continued, "This area will be more difficult. The Jews and the Arabs are true believers in their faith and will defend it to the death. One thing I did not count on, but considered a possibility, was them setting aside religious differences to join forces in opposition. Our threat of nuclear annihilation hasn't moved them into surrendering. I fear even a limited target strike would do nothing, or provoke a retaliatory strike. We don't have an accurate assessment of their nuclear weapons. Our strategy is to isolate the region. Containment and subsequent takeover. *This* is why religion is so dangerous to China. It is a rallying cry that draws fanatics, and you can't control fanatics. You can only kill them. My preference is to keep the region intact. If they do not surrender to our yoke, they'll leave us no choice. Is it not obvious that if we could topple the great America, we can conquer anyone? Again, the dangers of religion. The religious fanatics truly believe God is on their side."

Looking at the map of the Middle East, Chang said, "They will come to know that China is the new god."

NORTHERN MAINE

*There is no greater fury than the hate that is
fired in the white-hot coals of revenge.*

L AWRENCE "S PIKE" B LACKLOCK sat in the woods
still dark with night. A flickering pale yellow light
was given off by a small campfire he built, tucked into an
outcrop of rocks so as not to be seen. A percolating pot
of coffee was suspended over the fire. Squatting on the
ground still wet with the early morning dew, he poured
himself a cup using the speckled metallic blue mug his
wife had given him years before. She'd presented the mug
to him as a gift when he opened his wilderness camps. She
joked it would remind him of her every time he held the
cup to his lips. It was now all he had left of her. It was
his most cherished possession. As he lifted the cup, loving
memories of her whirled through his mind.

Around him were his four soldiers still sleeping in black
hemp hammocks strung up between the trees. They were
alone except for the intermittent sounds of nocturnal animals, both predator and prey trying to survive. The occasional shriek and the dry rustle of thorn bushes were the
only other sounds that punctuated the eerily quiet night.
He was ever vigilant and didn't know how not to be anything else, always studying the shadows in the woods

knowing that any one of them could act as camouflage for Chinese troops. The forest floor was a blanket of soft, damp pine needles, which would keep their approach silent, but he knew he could rely on the distinctive screech of the great horned owl to alert him to any impending danger. He let his men sleep a little while longer. Lawrence and his soldiers had been living by the laws of the wilderness for three years now. They were all loners, men who, like him, had lost everything and everyone they loved at the hands of the brutal Chinese. These men were dedicated to Lawrence and followed his every command unquestioned. They respected his combat experience and his ability to navigate the wild, both unseen and unheard. They shared a common purpose...to seek revenge on the Chinese.

Spike was a compact man and had the lean, carved muscles of a leopard, and some would say he was every bit as dangerous, if not more so. He had the endurance and physical stamina of men half his age. His hair was closely clipped, short enough that you could not tell if he had yet begun to gray. His hands were hard and calloused as a chunk of a gnarled piece of oak, with the scars befitting a fighting soldier. He had a handsome face that showed great intelligence, but also fearlessness and inner toughness. His most striking feature was his steel-blue eyes. Beneath the eyes and the handsome rugged face was a man capable of extreme violence. Most women were initially drawn to his gaze then, sensing the violence beneath, would quickly back away. Every woman except Amy. Any alarm bells that Amy might have had about Lawrence were curiously silent. She loved him totally, accepted him for the man he was. He never lost his patience with her or raised his voice in anger. She never once feared him, but felt safe and secure for the first time in her life when nestled in his arms. The thought of her, and her death, was ever present in his mind. He was haunted by the thought that if she had left Miami just one day earlier, she might still be alive. The loss of his wife was an open, painful wound that would not heal. He did not want it to heal. He kept the red-hot embers of the memories of their life together stoked and burning intensely. It fueled his hatred for the Chinese.

Sleep did not come easy for him, and when it did come, it brought with it her terrible screams as the Chinese put her to death, as surely as if they pulled the trigger. In every dream, he was running toward her to save her, but his legs were mired down in mud as she looked at him with pleading eyes before they faded, giving up her life.

They had met in the north island of New Zealand. He was on leave from the American war in Afghanistan, nursing some broken ribs suffered on a covert mission. They met in a bar in Wellington. Amy was on a business trip from New York City, selling her line of expensive diamond watches. She sidled up to the crowded bar and took the empty seat next to him. He was surprised when she ordered two shots of Johnny Walker Blue, and when the bartender placed the two shots down, slid one next to him. Amy clinked her glass with his, and in one quick motion threw the shot down and ordered two more. She turned sideways on her stool, looking at him squarely in the face and said, "So what's your story, handsome?" *That* sort of stuff never happened to him. He was a loner in every sense of the term. He rarely dated, and when he did, the girl would inevitably break it off. His underlying anger and violence would first attract and then repel women. He made them nervous, like the lion that wasn't contained by the zoo bars anymore. There were the bad boys, and then there was Lawrence. He would have made a pet out of most of the men who *thought* they were bad.

He had reached a point where he didn't even try to connect with women. He had plenty of one- or two-night affairs but never let them go beyond that point. His world became a cold and lonely place, which was just fine by him.

They chattered about everything and nothing, and when the bartender announced last call they both were genuinely surprised that the evening had passed so quickly. She slid off her stool, took him by the hand, and invited him up to her room—a suite, really—at the posh Four Seasons Hotel across the street. He accepted with just a silent nod of his head.

When they arrived at the room, he didn't want her to turn on the lights. She let him undress her, and when he started to remove his own clothing, she stopped him, wanting to do it herself. Although the room was dark, with only minimal light streaming in from the open windows, he was embarrassed by the patchwork of scars on his body. As she slowly undressed him, she kissed each scar made by either a bullet or a knife and asked him to tell her the story behind each wound. He surprised himself by telling her. They began to make love softly, tentatively. They explored each other's bodies with great respect and tenderness. He had never experienced such lovemaking. For him, despite the many women, it was little more than the satisfaction of a primal, lustful urge. Ordinarily he would put on his clothes and be out the door the moment the sex act was finished. For the first time, he experienced an emotional connection, exhilarating and scaring him simultaneously. He didn't want to leave.

Lawrence wanted to know everything about her. As they lay in bed in each other's arms, she told him that she was from an Italian family in East Boston. Her parents owned and operated a small pizzeria and Italian restaurant. She was the oldest of three children and had two brothers, one a cop in New York, the other an immigration attorney in Washington DC. Her mother worked in the restaurant but pretty much stayed home to raise the kids. Her father, unlike the traditional Italian male at the time, encouraged Amy to go to college, telling her she could accomplish anything she set her mind to. When she was still a young child, he took her snowmobiling in Maine, another time on a helicopter ride in New Hampshire, and when she turned eighteen, he took her skydiving in western Massachusetts. She went to college at UConn, found she had an aptitude for business, and upon graduating with honors, went to work for a large marketing firm in New York City. After five years, she believed she was being stifled by the man who owned the firm. She left the security of a large salary, pension plan, and all the usual perks in order to strike out on her own. She now had a large office in Manhattan with a commanding view of the New York skyline but lived in a loft in Brooklyn in an old converted chocolate factory with her dog, Milo. Now, a few short years later, she headed a successful company with over fifty employees and with customers around the world.

"You live with a dog?"

"Milo. He's a mutt. After dating loser after loser, I gave up on men. It just was easier. And *he* never disappoints me," she said with a smile, then she leaned over and tugged at his earlobe. "Now what's your story, my handsome soldier?"

He told her. All of it. Surprising even him. He was born in New Zealand, an only child of a retired military officer and a mother who was a successful actress. He was a handful at an early age, revealing a willful independent streak. In order to instill discipline, his parents enrolled him in a highly rated boarding school, Saint Kevin's in Oamaru, until the age of fifteen, when the headmaster had advised his father he would be better served attending a military academy. He had a quiet, brooding disposition, a loner by nature, and when he was teased by his classmates, he responded with his fists. As a result of his last fight, the local mayor's son's nose was broken, and that, as they say, was that. He was asked to leave.

His father put him in the New Zealand Military Academy, and under the strict tutelage of the proctors, he flourished. He excelled at math and science, and became more than proficient at survival skills, hand-to-hand combat, communications, and weapons training. The fact that he preferred his own company allowed him to excel in solo settings. He played rugby for the New Zealand Under 21 team as a forward, and proudly wore the Black. His deft footwork and thrilling line breaks, plus a willingness to sacrifice his body, earned him the respect of both his teammates and adversaries. He earned his nickname, Spike, by spiking the ball defiantly in the defenders' faces when he scored a goal.

Upon graduation, he joined the New Zealand Army and was stationed at the Waiouru Army Base. There he became a commando in the intelligence division of the New Zealand Special Air Service and was recruited by the SAS. He was trained to be a sniper and taught to survive in harsh environments with only his wits to keep him alive. Soon after, he was transferred to the base in Hobsonville. Although his country was not involved in any conflicts, they would almost always fight side by side with the United States. The Kiwis loved a good fight. He volunteered and was deployed to the Helmut province in Afghanistan. For two tours, Lawrence operated deep behind enemy lines without backup or radio, bringing instant death to Taliban leaders. No one was safe from his sniper rifle. His stealth and ability to kill from long range earned him the nickname of the White Ghost. He became a legend, a myth in the mountains. Hardened enemy soldiers would speak of him in hushed tones, as if the mere mention of his name would summon him like a demon from hell bringing death with him. A large bounty was placed on his head, but no one was eager to try to collect it.

He found out he was very good at killing.

Amy and Lawrence spent the weekend together and were inseparable. She extended her stay in order to explore the countryside of New Zealand with him. They traveled to Oamaru to see the blue penguin colony; he bought her a cute, small stuffed penguin which she promptly named Gus, after a German shepherd she had and loved as a child. They dined at the historic Pig & Whistle, and when they walked in, there was a moment that the bartender considered throwing Lawrence out. Lawrence had forgotten that two years previous, he had gotten into a brawl with three Aussie soldiers, putting two of them in the local hospital. The only reason Lawrence wasn't arrested was because of the stripes of the SAS on his shoulders. Evidently the bartender did not forget the incident, but Amy cooed and smoothed things over. The barkeep still kept a wary eye on Lawrence and felt infinitely better when they walked out the door.

They went to Queenstown and stayed at a small B&B, hiking the beach hand in hand in the morning, and making love in the afternoon. They drove to the Kawarau Bridge made famous by Kiwi legend AJ Hackett, who years earlier decided to attach a bungee cord to his feet and jumped 142 feet off a bridge, hoping the rubber cord would hold so he wouldn't plunge to his death. Now the same man ran a commercial business where hundreds came daily just to watch the few brave or crazy people repeating his daring feat. Munching on a basket of golden fried fish, Amy said, "So whaddaya think? Want to jump?" Lawrence looked at this little pretty girl with amazement. "No. I do not. *No!* I'm deployed in a hostile country where people are always trying to either blow me up or shoot me. I have *no* intention of dying because some idiot attendant didn't tie the cord around my ankles properly!"

Amy looked at the small line of people buying tickets and said, "Well I'm going," and leaving Lawrence speechless, headed off to buy her ticket. Five minutes later, he watched in shock as Amy climbed the platform that hovered over the rock-strewn Kawarau River below. With a wave and not a moment's hesitation, she swan dived off the narrow platform. *Now this is some kind of girl,* he thought with pride.

The next day they checked out of the B&B and took a guided tour of five of the premium vineyards in Central Otago, a beautiful region marked with rugged snow-capped mountains and picturesque alpine lakes, where they sipped wine and sampled the local cheeses. They continued driving south, sadly knowing that the time was quickly approaching when they must say good-bye, something neither one of them wished to acknowledge. Lawrence's leave was almost up, and he was due to report back to his company. Amy appeared content to extend her vacation even further, not wanting this dream to end. She laughed to herself that she had to fly almost twenty-three hours around the world to find a man she could love and a country that was the most beautiful she had ever seen.

Their driving continued down the coast, along a scenic road lined with trees, leaves the color of a deep jade, still glistening with the morning's dew. Rounding a bend, they pulled into the tiny hamlet of Lake Tekapo. There, perched on the shore of the lake, was the Church of the Good Shepherd. It stood alone, built in homage to God. Unlike some other churches that reflected wealth and power, it was a small, simple building constructed of wooden beams and stone, built on a foundation of rough, unchipped rocks, with heavy wooden shingles for a roof and adorned with a simple wooden cross. The original builders wanted a church to reflect the simple carpenter whose teachings of love and forgiveness opened the kingdom of heaven to all.

From their car they watched as a small wedding with no more than a dozen people was concluding. The priest was giving his final blessings as the newly married couple was exiting the doorway in a rainstorm of rice thrown by family and well-wishers. The wedding party gathered around the newly married husband and wife, then walked to the inn across the street, where the celebration would continue. Amy took Lawrence's hand and went inside. The church overlooked a still and serene Lake Tekapo. They walked to the window and looked out; neither a boat nor person could be seen, and the water was as clear and still as an enormous flat piece of blue glass stretching out for miles. They stood there, motionless, barely aware of their breathing. Neither Amy nor Lawrence considered themselves a devoutly religious person. They believed in God and went to the obligatory weddings and funerals, but that day, they felt God's love flow into them. Almost simultaneously, they turned to each other and said, "Let's get married."

Amy rustled up the priest, a large man with an ample belly and sporting an unruly shock of grey hair, an infectious laugh. Rather than being dismayed at the lack of planning, he was delighted that this young couple standing before him, so obviously in love, wished to swear their vows before God in his humble church. Truly God's love had inspired them. If the town had not been so small (population 436—and *that* was in the summer), such a spontaneous wedding might not have been possible. Even the necessary paperwork was handled by the priest, so Amy and Lawrence were able to bypass a closed Town Hall.

"Well it *is* unusual, I know, but Bob, the town clerk, is often away fishing. We both thought it best if I handled all the matters tied to the church. And as luck has it, Bob went fishing two days ago and has yet to return!" The priest joked in a low voice, "Sometimes he likes to bring a bottle of fine Irish whiskey with him. To get away from his wife, you know," giving a knowing wink.

While Amy was filling out the necessary forms, Lawrence walked to the local market and bought a bouquet of fresh flowers and managed to cajole a young man sitting outside the store strumming his guitar to walk back to the church with him and play at their wedding service. In just under an hour, Amy, Lawrence, the priest, and one happy young man whom Lawrence had thrown a $100 bill for thirty minutes work playing a guitar, assembled in front of the altar with the golden sunlight shining in. Before God and man they pledged their love for one another.

After two blissful days at the local inn, where they barely got out of bed, Lawrence drove his new wife back to the airport. He would put in his papers and receive an honorable discharge from the SAS. His commander said it was sad to lose such a good soldier, but joked it was better to lose Lawrence to a wife than to the Taliban. Besides, the enemy didn't know he was retiring, so you never know, they would probably still be looking over their shoulders for the White Ghost and the death he brought.

Amy would fly back and inform Milo the dog that he was getting a new dad. Lawrence would tidy up a few things—not much, really, as he had little in the way of material possessions—say good-bye to family and friends, and join his wife in New York City.

After just a few short months in New York, Lawrence was climbing the walls. Life in the city just didn't agree with him. It was too noisy. He'd take Milo on long walks—too long, Milo thought—and joined a gym to stay in peak shape, but he missed the solitude that only nature brought. On Amy's suggestion, they explored the Adirondack Mountains to the north, and she pushed him to start a business teaching wilderness survival skills. It would get him out of the city and get him back doing something he loved. They bought two hundred acres in a remote area of beautiful countryside. Lawrence hand-built five small log cabins by a stream, and the New Zealand Wilderness School was born.

It was an immediate hit. He taught both men and women, weekend warriors from Wall Street, how to start a fire with damp wood, make a shelter, use a bent pin to catch fish, and what berries they could and couldn't eat while hiking in the woods. "Remember, if a bird eats it, you can too," he advised. He set up a pistol and rifle range and taught gun safety and the proper way to shoot. The clients loved going on long hikes with Lawrence pointing out the local flora and fauna. He reveled in the looks of wonder when these urban dwellers would come across a deer or porcupine. There were no land lines for phones, certainly no cell towers, no fax machines or laptops, and after an initial panic, his clients found that once free from their electric collars, they loved every minute of it. Especially knowing that at the end of the weekend they would be going home to all the creature comforts each had left behind.

His clients would head home on late Sunday morning after a breakfast of fresh coffee, juice, ham, bacon, eggs, home fries, and toast cooked over an open campfire. Lawrence usually waited until Tuesday to head home in order to stay an extra day and get in some trout fishing. But all that was gone now. Ever since the austerity measures were put in place by the government, the weekend warriors stayed at home and business completely dried up. As conditions in the city became progressively worse, he even considered moving to New Zealand, but Amy didn't want to leave her father. Her mother had passed some years ago. Her dad had been recently diagnosed with dementia and was living in an assisted living facility in Miami. So together they decided that Amy would fly down to Miami and pick up her father, and they would all move to the wilderness camp in the Adirondacks until the madness subsided.

A week before the Chinese detonated the ten NEMPs across America, Lawrence dropped Amy off at LaGuardia airport on a flight bound for Miami, where she would collect her father and then return. Lawrence drove up to the wilderness camps to bring in some provisions for the long winter and add to the pile of firewood already cut.

It was on such a beautiful fall day, when the leaves in the Adirondacks began to turn crimson and gold, and thoughts turned to carving pumpkins and sipping mugs of hot apple cider, that the Chinese invaded America.

Lawrence drove his usual way home, taking Route 56, which ran from his wilderness camp in Childwold along the fast flowing Raquette River. He connected with Route 30, which spilled into the tiny hamlet of Blue Mountain Lake. He fiddled with the radio as he drove, finding a sports station. He drove down the road a piece enjoying the scenery He looked at his cell phone resting in the holder on the dashboard. He switched on the power to call Amy to let her know he was on his way home and access any other messages he might have. When he reached her, she was at the airport terminal ready to board the plane. She laughed at what a handful her father had become and said that she might just have to tie him to a tree once she got him up there. They said their usual good-byes and hung up.

About an hour into his drive, Lawrence pulled into John's Bait Store, which also had a small breakfast counter and reasonably fresh coffee—if you considered six-hour-old, burnt coffee fresh—to grab some bacon and eggs without Amy around to nag him about eating healthy. He shut off the engine, opened his truck door, and walked around the dirt parking lot. He walked in the store, clanging the overhead bell announcing his arrival. He found John, his wife Mary, and a few customers huddled around the small ham radio that sat next to the powdered sugar doughnuts on the counter. "What is going on?" he asked the group.

"Chinese attacked us today. Set off some electronic bombs across America. Can you believe that?"

Lawrence immediately called Amy's cell phone to warn her not to get on that plane. The "on" button lit up red indicating he had power, but he couldn't get a signal. *Strange*, he thought, as a sense of uneasiness crept in his mind. Lawrence tried to control the rising panic in his chest, remembering his training. He listened to the reports coming in of massive damage across the country, but most disturbing were the accounts of planes falling out of the sky.

Lawrence stared at the radio but didn't hear any sounds as his only thoughts were with his wife. He looked at his watch and knew. He'd finally found himself a life worth living, and the Chinese had stolen it from him.

Lawrence was going back to war.

Fall 2025

WASHINGTON DC

I T WAS THE most perfect sneak attack launched on a nation, and the most treacherous.

One year earlier, in October of 2024, China stunned the world when it requested the return of the 19 trillion dollars it had lent to the United States. Quite simply, the Chinese wanted their money back. It was a loan, was it not? Loans are written with a clause giving the lender a legal right to call in the note. It's always in the fine print. China's loan to the United States was no different; however, recalling such a large loan rarely, if ever, was done. At least, not until now.

President Mann attempted to negotiate with the Chinese Chairman Chang, but his efforts were met with steely denials. The United States did not have the 19 trillion— no nation did. In order to save the value and integrity of the US dollar, the government instituted unprecedented austerity measures. It immediately suspended payments to all social programs. Recipients of Social Security benefits were given chits, which in reality were of little or no value. Government disability programs suffered the same fate. Payments to Medicare and Medicaid were curtailed, which forced hospitals to suspend medical treatment to some of the nation's most needy citizens. Doctor's offices were shuttered. Insulin-dependent diabetics found that there was no Humalog to be found. Ambulances remained parked in hospital lots. Food banks shut down, and runs on groceries and supplies at every local store were the norm. Unable to get resupplied from their vendors, gas stations closed. Banks were flooded with customers demanding their money, unaware that banks routinely kept only small amounts of cash on hand. Angry depositors, who did not understand why their withdrawal slips could not be honored, rioted. At a small bank in Hattiesburg, Indiana, the bank manager was dragged into the street and severely beaten. Confusion led to panic, and panic led to violence in the streets. Martial law was declared, but without a funded National Guard or army, it could not be enforced. Overnight, America fell into the abyss of anarchy.

A new law emerged from the chaos: firearms, and those willing to use them, ruled.

In an attempt to remediate the situation, the US government raised interest rates on Treasury Bills by an unprecedented 4 percent. However, there were few takers. Foreign countries that normally hedged their own currency with T-Bills could not afford to buy more should the US economy collapse. If the post office had still been in operation, people would have been receiving notices that their credit cards, adjustable rate mortgages, and loans were either being called in, or their monthly payment amount had doubled or tripled. Congress ordered the Treasury to print more money, which only served to further devalue an already crippled dollar.

On their end, the Chinese made good on their threats and seized American property at every opportunity. All American assets in China were frozen, regardless of whether they were privately owned. The Chinese negotiated for the United States to turn over five of their ten large navy aircraft carriers; thirty-two of their destroyer battleships; twenty-four of their fifty-three fast attack subs; an assortment of frigates, cruisers, patrol and support ships; two of the four guided missile subs; and finally, ten of their ballistic missile subs. As a stopgap measure, the United States complied, hoping to appease the Chinese.

In addition to these concessions, the Chinese demanded, not requested, that all Aquacade satellites, or SIGINT, that were used by the CIA to monitor intercepted Chinese communications be immediately deactivated. These were configured as midsized satellites that utilized an umbrella-like reflecting dish twenty meters in diameter, intercepted microwave relays, and had the ability to pick up a house-hold conversation in rural China. They stated that this was a violation of Chinese airspace. Again, the United States complied.

In return, the Chinese agreed to (1) sign a non-aggression pact; (2) join NATO; and (3) give the United States more time and better terms to renegotiate the balance of the 19 trillion dollar loan. The Americans had no choice but to acquiesce to the draconian terms. In the short months since the enactment of the austerity program, the country was imploding while the world watched.

America signed the agreement, and tried to piece herself back together.

But China wasn't finished.

CHINA

C HINA TRANSFORMED SCIENCE fiction into reality.
A little-known historical fact enabled the successful Japanese sneak attack on Pearl Harbor on December 7, 1941. While the element of surprise certainly played a critical part in the nefarious Japanese plot, it was the clandestine development of a shallow-water torpedo that made the attack a success. Until 1941, in order to have an effective detonation, a torpedo needed to be launched by plane and reach a depth of seventy-five to one hundred twenty-five feet. The depth of the American fleet at Pearl Harbor was thirty feet. Thus while the US military thought they might suffer an air attack, no bombs could reach the vulnerable area under the great warships' armor belt that lay beneath the water line. Clearly they were wrong. The subsequent attack crippled the Pacific Fleet, but also triggered the adverse effect of bringing America into the war.

Like Japan, Xi Chang knew that he had a historic opportunity to not only cripple the United States but to completely annihilate it. He knew that by doing so, China could effectively rule the world, not just America. The world. Other nations' economies would be in shambles, and no one singular nation could match either China's military might or its willingness to accept a great loss of its soldiers in attaining global domination. The current obstacle was the vast amount of American nuclear weapons. Even with a military that had been reduced time and time again by its spineless politicians, America remained poised as a nuclear behemoth. Chang had to figure out how to neutralize America's nuclear might and crush its resolve.

Long before China requested the United States pay back its loans, it built a secret manufacturing facility nestled deep in the rugged plateaus of the Qilian Shan mountain range, hidden from the roving eyes of US satellites. The Chinese developed the latest fabrication machinery operated by state-of-the-art lasers. There, it brought its best and brightest engineers and scientists to develop the first nuclear electromagnetic pulse bomb, or NEMP, using unique components that would not emit a radiation signature which could be detected by American sensors. Until now, EMPs were small, ineffective, and viewed as "science fiction" and generally deemed impractical as a weapon by most of the world's leading scientists.

The EMP was a bomb that set off bursts of electromagnetic radiation, causing voltage surges and disrupting normal electrical connections. The effect was similar to a lightning bolt striking a house and frying the television and toaster that were plugged into a normal household electrical outlet. It would cause a very brief but very intense spike in the electromagnetic field. This produced an extremely high-voltage surge that would damage any sensitive electronic components in its radius, plugged in or not.

Small prototypes of these bombs had been tested by many governments as early as the 1950s. Each country had hoped to be the first to develop the next great and devastating military weapon. However, in order to be effective on a large scale, the bomb's detonation had to interact with the natural existing magnetic field that surrounded

Earth's atmosphere, which would amplify the electromagnetic pulse waves. Even if scientists could solve this problem, channeling a bomb to affect a single country was not possible. It would be similar to setting off a nuclear explosion high in space. The radiation fallout would settle over both friendly and hostile nations. After extensive testing, it was shelved as impossible.

Until the Chinese figured out a way to make it work.

The Chinese went smaller. Rather than trying to duplicate the ten-megaton EMP bombs the United States tested in 1954, the Chinese developed a one-megaton NEMP bomb, small enough to fit into a household kitchen refrigerator, yet still fifty times more powerful than the bombs set off in Hiroshima and Nagasaki. Encased in a titanium shell, a bomb this size detonated at an altitude of five thousand feet over Kansas would affect most of the central continental US. It was the largest weapons breakthrough since the Manhattan Project. Xi authorized the immediate production of the weapon.

The difficulty of smuggling these bombs into the United States had been overcome years ago. As China began to export its people and capital around the world, it found a foothold in Mexico because it shared a border with the United States. If Mexico alone had been selected, Homeland Security would have been on red alert. Because Mexico was just one of twenty-six countries receiving Chinese workers and financial aid, it didn't raise one eyebrow. At that time, America had good relations with China, and the only threat emanating from Mexico was the illegal drug trafficking across the US-Mexican border.

In order to prepare for its attack on the United States, China established a working relationship with the Zetas, Mexico's largest and most deadly drug cartel. The Zetas were composed of former military personnel known for their extreme violence and hatred of the United States. They were the logical choice to partner with the Chinese. The Chinese were able to provide the Zetas with something more important to them than money: i.e., weapons, an arsenal of modern assault rifles, grenades, and land mines—any and all military equipment the Zetas would need to dominate and tip the balance of power in their favor with other drug cartels.

The Zetas operated in Nuevo Laredo, a border city in northeastern Mexico surrounded by hills scorched by the unrelenting sun. Thousands of trucks traveled its main highways delivering both legal and illegal merchandise to the United States. It is one of the busiest land ports in all of Latin America. Its largest trading partner— unofficially, of course—was the State of Texas. Most of the Border Patrol agents manning the border checkpoints were chosen especially for their fluency in English and Spanish. Some of them still had family living in Mexico, which fostered a vulnerability to the violent drug cartels. There was an old saying in the Border Patrol when it came to the Zetas: it's better to accept their silver than taste their lead. The Chinese chose Nuevo Laredo to set up shop by purchasing an existing nondescript grey slab concrete building that manufactured refrigerators sold to the United States. There wasn't anything to set this building apart from the many similar such structures in which American appliances and televisions were built except for the unusually excessive amount of high-resolution motion detection security cameras and the heavily armed guards patrolling the razor wire-enclosed yard with attack dogs. The Chinese assembled the parts necessary to build the

NEMPs in the back of the factory in a sealed area that was strictly off limits to all but a select few.

The Chinese had a symbiotic relationship with the Zetas. Apart from the money the Chinese paid to the Zetas to bribe and intimidate the local Mexican authorities, they were able to offer the drug cartel a way to ship their drugs into the United States hidden inside the appliances they manufactured. All that was needed was for the Zetas to arrange for the border crossing—something the Zetas were very good at and had already been doing successfully for years.

The Chinese contracted for the Zetas to smuggle in ten refrigerators, a feat neither large nor difficult since most American household appliances were now being manufactured in Mexico, thanks to the NAFTA treaty. The Zetas were paid for not knowing that each appliance contained a single NEMP. Only Chinese drivers were permitted to load and drive these modified refrigerators across the border. The Zetas scheduled drivers to pass through the border crossing at a specific time and place when a cooperative and well-bribed border patrol agent would wave them through. From there, the trucks were driven to a nondescript storage facility that stood with hundreds of other similar buildings in the warehouse district of Laredo, Texas.

From this location, they would be transported in the familiar brown UPS trucks. Thanks to the relaxed restrictions on foreign governments buying land, buildings, and businesses, a Chinese straw company acting for the Chinese government bought UPS for 2.1 trillion dollars, and in turn, bought themselves the perfect covert delivery system for clandestine weapons and men. Brown delivers.

The second stage of the Chinese attack on the United States was ready.

UNITED STATES

THE DAY AMERICA fell was just another ordinary day. Well, the new ordinary, anyway.

Chaos reigned in the streets, and because the sanitation department had been dismantled, garbage piled up high. Along with the usual fast food wrappers from McDonalds and broken whisky and beer bottles, rats ran rampant. Even more disconcerting was the random disposal of corpses in broad daylight. Some natural deaths were hastened due to the lack of medical care after the hospitals' closings. Without ambulances to remove the bodies, they often were just wrapped in sheets or blankets and then dumped unceremoniously at the sidewalk curb. Mild heart attacks that were once treatable turned fatal. Other victims had been beaten to death or simply shot trying to hang on to a precious bag full of groceries. Stores were closed, and any supplies they may have had were looted a long time ago. Guns and bullets were the new gold. Groups of men banded together, desperate to protect their families, and fought for food and medicine. Gun battles raged in the streets. Those lucky enough to have cars and full tanks of gas drove into the countryside on raids, where they were met, more often than not, by farmers with their own guns and families to protect.

The US government was powerless to intervene. Most elected politicians stayed out of sight, especially after a mob stormed Congress and hung the fourteen Congressmen they found hiding in chambers. The president was locked deep in his bunker far beneath the White House with his Cabinet and a battalion of heavily armed marines to protect him. If he had shown his face, he certainly would have been assassinated. Most people knew it was the decades of ineffectual, corrupt leadership of the government, the inability to stop the out-of-control spending, and the paralysis between the Democratic and Republican parties that brought them to this day. The day of reckoning had arrived.

At noon on the day of October 14, a day that the Americans were celebrating as Columbus Day, Chairman Chang gave the order to detonate the NEMPs. All ten bombs had already been delivered to strategic sites around the United States. Each bomb had such a large blast radius that it was critical for them to be spread out equally between the ten largest-populated cites. The bombs were brought on board UPS planes, along with other cargo. The pilots, all Chinese agents who had long resided in the United States and had attained American citizenship, took off on preselected flight paths. Even knowing that death was imminent, the Chinese agents participated willingly. They knew that their families would be well taken care of and that each would be forever remembered as one of the ten patriotic comrades that brought America to her knees.

It was thought that the most difficult location, the one that took the most planning and deception, was getting a bomb in NORAD. As it turned out, it was much easier than expected.

The acronym NORAD stood for North American Aerospace Defense. It provided aerospace warning and was the heart of the defensive system for both the United States and Canada. NORAD used the most advanced computer technology, similar to the Doppler radar system but even more sophisticated. Through its BMEWS, or Ballistic Missile Early Warning System, it was set up to spot heat signatures and exhaust plumes that would indicate a missile launch anywhere in the world. All this information was cross-referenced and shared with the American and Canadian civilian and military air traffic control. This computer system was hardwired and located deep underground and connected to a worldwide system of sensors and orbiting satellites. From these sophisticated computers, an American president could give the order to launch a nuclear attack.

To protect NORAD from a physical assault that would, in effect, blind the eyes and ears of North America, NORAD was built into the Cheyenne Mountain Air Force Station in Colorado. It was a bunker buried so deep in the mountain and so heavily fortified, it could withstand a direct hit from a nuclear attack. What protected NORAD was also its Achilles' heel. Like the fabled city of Troy, a wooden horse would take it down. Because NORAD was constructed hundreds of feet beneath the earth and located far away from any major city or town, NORAD relied on a steady stream of outside vendors, who had passed strict government security clearances in order to be able to deliver the routinely needed supplies of paper, food, ink cartridges, laundry services, medical supplies, and even the occasional pizza for the brass. So while NORAD searched the skies for any visible threat to the safety and security of North America on this fateful day, the guards waved through a familiar brown UPS truck that had been making deliveries to that location for years.

The wooden horse had arrived, and today, it would be making a *very* special delivery.

Each of the ten bombs was rigged with a timer (the various time zones were accounted for), and precisely at noon was detonated by a Toshiba Satellite A135 laptop computer, one easily purchased at any Staples or OfficeMax. In a small apartment building on Park Ave in Brooklyn, a small, compact man sat on a plain white couch he purchased from Pottery Barn. Poised over a laptop computer, he typed in the code which activated the sequence that sent out a signal to each bomb, while he sipped his green tea. Having completed his mission, he smiled knowingly as he unfurled the abridged version of the Wenhui Xinmin, China's daily newspaper, and nibbled on his edamame.

At exactly noon on October 14, 2025, a brisk fall day with just a slight chilly breeze, ten nuclear electromagnetic pulse bombs detonated simultaneously across America. Over the populated cities of New York, Chicago, San Francisco, Dallas, and Seattle; to the smaller towns of Lancaster, Pennsylvania; Minot, South Dakota; Aspen, Colorado; and Alamogordo, New Mexico; to the small villages of Amherst, Massachusetts; Lake Charles, Louisiana; and Roseau, Minnesota; and extending five hundred miles into the northern reaches of Mexico; ceramic insulators on overhead electrical power lines exploded, blasting violently and completely frying all circuits. Power lines burst away from the telephone poles that held them and toppled to the ground, crashing on cars parked below. The fuses and gas-filled overvoltage protectors were no match for the highly charged electrons traveling at 90 percent of the speed of light causing violent surges in underground power lines, resulting in massive fires in power plants all across North America. The only locations that were not affected were the heavily forested areas in the border regions along the United States and Canada, where the towering evergreen trees blocked the microwaves.

In a period of minutes, every television, radio, microwave oven, refrigerator, toaster, electric light, ceiling fan, air conditioner, heater, and every other electrical appliance ceased to work. The electrical system in cars, trains, buses, boats, helicopters, and motorcycles stopped dead in their tracks. Airplanes fell out of the sky in fiery crashes. Hospitals, schools, police and fire stations, and television and radio studios lost their power. Nearby houses were set ablaze. In Kentucky, thirty-eight thoroughbred race horses were burned alive when their stable turned into an inferno. Due to the previous austerity measures, there were no fire trucks or firefighters to respond.

This was not a temporary glitch where the system would reboot itself and you could buy a new coffee pot and plug it in. For the most part, America's whole vast electrical power grid was destroyed. The Internet, a mysterious marvel of technology, is not wireless as believed, but a series of cables all connected from one massive router to another, joined together at various exchange points. The two main junctions where the transatlantic cables met coming into the United States were located in Lower Manhattan and Ashburn, Virginia. When the NEMPs detonated, the large routers with the multi-blinking lights were completely destroyed, along with the cables coming in along the ocean floor of the Atlantic. The Internet collapsed.

People attempting to use their cell phones, thinking they were linked by some mysterious cloud in space, only had dead air, as every cell tower had erupted into flames. The loss of life was serious, as any loss of life is, but was small compared to the damage done to the country's infrastructure. The NEMP attack wiped out physical electrical lines, and the shock waves destroyed the complex circuitry of sensitive electronics.

When the clock struck twelve in NORAD, the bomb detonated inside the nuclear protected bunker. Being inside, completely enclosed by solid rock and heavily reinforced steel doors, the NEMP completely destroyed the most heavily protected United States military and civilian electronic systems ever devised. The loss of life was total. Without anywhere for the bomb's blast to go, it was confined and reverberated within the bunker's walls, killing every man and woman inside. Instantaneously every military ship, plane, submarine, and foreign base lost all communication with NORAD. Communications ceased with orbiting US satellites. The White House and the military's most secure sat phones only had dead air. Nuclear-powered fast-attack submarines armed with nuclear-tipped intercontinental missiles held their position, not knowing if America had been attacked (or even, for that matter, by whom) as all communications went unanswered. Terrorists from the Middle East? The Russians? The Chinese? While they may have had their suspicions, nuclear submarine commanders are commanded by the rules of engagement, not personal assumptions, so they held their course, awaiting orders. Orders that would never come.

While the Chinese really didn't care how many Americans they killed, they *did* need to kill as many as possible to make a point, knowing those surviving Americans would be a resilient, scrappy bunch. The Chinese wanted to take over the United States intact. They knew that a vast number of its citizens owned firearms, so they needed to provide a strong deterrent, and at the same time, give pause to a heavily armed populace. China needed America's valuable natural resources and its vast landmass for its own people to expand, so they took great care not to implode America's sixty-five nuclear power plants. After all, making the United States uninhabitable did not serve the needs of China. Each nuclear power plant was shielded from radiation in the event of an inside leak or break, and that precaution saved it from a meltdown when the Chinese attacked. They certainly could have sent their UPS trucks into each facility; they had the bomb-making capacity to produce NEMPs at will, but they wanted to keep the nuclear power plants to generate power for themselves. While all the sensitive electronics were damaged, the core remained safe.

The Chinese weren't done yet.

October 14, 2025

WASHINGTON DC

5 p.m.

THE WHITE HOUSE went dark at noon. No one knew what had happened, first hoping and then praying it was a local blackout only affecting DC. The lights and phone lines went down along with the computers. The Joint Chiefs of Staff, especially those charged with Homeland Security, reported nervously that they had been unable to reach any of their local commanders. Worse, NORAD was dark. More disturbing than bad news was no news. It seemed that the eyes and ears of America were sealed shut.

This came on the heels of the country's attempt to maintain order in the wake of the previous fiscal chaos. President Mann assembled his Cabinet to assess the damage just as his secretary informed him that the Chinese ambassador was there to see him.

"Show him in immediately," President Mann barked.

Deng Xiaoping, the ambassador to China, was shown into the Oval Office and stood quietly and respectfully in front of President Mann's desk. He ignored the hostile looks from the attending Cabinet members, and instead handed the president a rosewood box with the seal of China engraved on its top.

"Mr. President, I was instructed to give you this secure satellite phone that will enable you to speak directly to Chairman Chang. He will be calling you momentarily."

No sooner than he spoke those words, a soft ringing sound emerged from the box.

"Please, Mr. President. It is Chairman Chang for you."

President Mann opened the box to find a 32-bit wireless sat phone that was directly linked to an orbiting Chinese overhead satellite. It was one of the few phones that still worked in America.

"Mr. President, I will come right to the point. We have crippled your country. As of twelve noon today, we have completely destroyed your energy infrastructure..."

"This is an act of *war! Have you forgotten that we have thousands of nuclear missiles aimed at your country as we speak?*" said President Mann, feeling himself losing control as he yelled into the phone.

"Actually you *don't,* Mr. President. NORAD was completely destroyed, rendering your nuclear subs dead in the water. The remaining 7,000 ICBMs were likewise rendered ineffective by the detonation of our NEMPs. There're as useless as the silos that house them. The circuitry in every missile was destroyed by the blast, and even if the missiles weren't destroyed, NORAD no longer exists to send the launch codes. Your ability to communicate with your military via satellite no longer exists."

"What do you want?" the president asked tersely, trying to keep the fear he felt from raising his tone.

"Since, Mr. President, you were so quick to threaten a nuclear strike—which, I might add, I expected—I will get right to the point. I want the complete and unconditional surrender of the United States to the People's Republic of China. We demand that within two hours, or 7 p.m. EST, you will turn over all your launch codes and the locations of your nuclear subs. You will inform all branches of your military to stand down. At 7 p.m. you will receive my delegation and surrender yourself and your full cabinet to them."

"This is an outrage! The world will not stand for this unilateral aggression against a peaceful nation! And if we refuse?"

"I fully expect you to refuse, Mr. President. That is why in one hour from now, at 6 p.m. EST, we will launch two nuclear strikes within the boundaries of the United States. This will make our demand for your surrender perfectly clear."

"Wait..."

"Then, if we do not have your complete, unconditional surrender, we will launch the rest of our nuclear missiles from our subs that surround your coast. Every major city in the United States will be destroyed, and the fallout from the nuclear radiation will make them uninhabitable for one hundred years. America will cease to exist. The choice is yours. Two hours, Mr. President."

"Wait! We can talk! We can come to an arrangement..."

"No arrangement, Mr. President. Surrender in two hours or have the death of millions of Americans on your hands."

"Then stop the attack in one hour. Give us time to respond, for God's sake!"

"There is no God, Mr. President, and I will not stop the attack. Two of your cites will cease to exist after six o'clock. My delegation is already in Washington and will call upon you at seven. At that time you will be presented with a formal surrender document. You will sign it, and you, your Cabinet, and the members of your family will present themselves for detention. Seven o'clock, Mr. President."

"Tell me, then, which two cities?"

"You'll see soon enough, Mr. President."

With that, Xi Chang terminated the connection. He was not bluffing about the impending nuclear attack; in fact, he had already given the orders. He selected Miami and San Diego for destruction. The cities were far enough away from the nuclear power plants in those states so as not to destroy them, but large enough to cause a massive loss of life. This was of no concern to Chang. Fewer Americans he had to deal with. He had no doubt the bombing would bring the surrender of the United States to him, but he had no compunction about launching the full nuclear strike if they didn't. He would have preferred not to contaminate two major cities with the fallout from the radiation, but he knew it was necessary to force the United States' surrender. Did the Americans not do the same thing to the Japanese at the end of WWII? Besides, Chang could live without Miami and San Diego. He took a sip from his steaming mug of tea and sat back to watch the clock on his desk. Fifty-three minutes to detonation.

WASHINGTON DC

5:10 p.m.

T HE PRESIDENT SAT stunned in the Oval Office. In just one day—six hours, really—the Republic that stood for over two centuries as the world's protector of human rights, with the strongest economy and the largest military in the world, collapsed.

Turning to his Chief of Staff he asked, "How could this happen?"

"Mr. President, apparently the Chinese were able to create nuclear electromagnetic pulse bombs small enough to smuggle into the US. How they brought them into our country and infiltrated NORAD remains to be seen. Until now this technology was deemed not possible. But by doing so, and detonating them above our airspace, they wiped out virtually every electronic data line and machine that relied on electronics…in a nutshell, everything. Everything is down. The Internet has collapsed, and there is no way for us to communicate with the American public, or for them to communicate with each other."

"How can I address the nation…"

"You can't. I would normally suggest you attempt to reach every military base by sat phone and inform them of the situation, but because the Chinese took out NORAD, that is no longer a possibility."

"Did this affect all of the US?"

"Pretty much, sir. Some rural parts, along our border of Canada, were hit, but not totally. Any areas that were heavily forested are probably okay. It's just too early to tell, but it doesn't look good. We're not getting any communication out of NORAD at all. All of our military bases that had sat phones were affected, and they're not reporting in. It appears all our communication and electronic equipment has been destroyed."

"Loss of life?"

"Again, sir, hard to tell. Nowhere near what it would have been if they were all nuclear atomic bombs."

"Ladies and gentlemen, I need your best analysis as to a course of action, and I need it now!" the president said, looking at the stunned faces surrounding him.

"Mr. President," the Joint Chiefs replied after huddling together for a brief moment, "The United States is completely vulnerable. Every military aircraft, tank, and ship that is on US ground or anchored offshore has most likely been rendered inoperable. We have no defense, Mr. President. While we certainly have ground troops available, the Chinese have the complete upper hand. Not to mention, they appear completely willing to use nuclear force. Without a way to communicate to our troops, we would be fighting completely blind with our hands tied behind our backs."

"Can we respond with a nuclear attack of our own?"

"No, sir. Not really. We do have attack subs off the Chinese coast, but with the safety protocols in place to avoid a mis-launch, and with our communications down, they would have to verify the attack code...if we could even get it to them, which we can't. By the time they do that, we would be well past the 7 p.m. deadline. The Chinese have shown their resolve, and I for one, Mr. President, have no doubt that they will launch the rest of their nukes if we don't comply."

President Mann sat in his chair knowing what he had to do. He could not suffer the destruction of his country by nuclear attack. He was sick to his stomach, and he was furious, but he was resigned to the fact that he would be the last sitting president of the United States, a country he loved but would be no more.

"At seven, we will receive the Chinese delegation. I will unconditionally surrender the United States to China. I will ask for peaceful terms for our citizens. That is all. I would suggest you go to your individual offices and remove what personal items you may have. There will be no time to destroy documents. Go."

MIAMI

6 p.m.

MIAMI WAS A city divided; for the uber rich it offered glitzy South Beach nightclubs and fine dining. You could order freshly caught stone crabs at Joe's Crab Shack and indulge in a bottle of Dom Perignon for a cool three hundred dollars. Oceanfront mansions and sixty-foot yachts docked at their own private piers were common. For the most part, those lavishing in this lifestyle were white.

Jack Gresophie was a retired CEO of New York Life Insurance Company. He started his career at the bottom, hustling small life insurance policies to returning soldiers starting a family. Born to a working class family, he believed in the value of life insurance. When he was a young man in high school, his favorite uncle died suddenly of a heart attack, leaving a young wife, two boys, and no insurance. He watched his father take on a second job delivering newspapers at night to help support them. Jack was a true believer in what he did.

He advanced through the ranks—first he was a sales manager, then office manager, VP, president, and finally CEO. He stayed until he turned sixty-five and retired. His wife, Maryann, was the retired Chancellor of Education for the State of New York. She was also one incredible golfer, and the only member of the prestigious Willow Golf and Country Club to ever record two holes-in-one on the challenging Fazio-designed course.

Their family raised, they decided to leave the bitter cold and snow of New York for the sunshine of Miami. Both avid sailors, they bought a sleek, sixty-foot mahogany sailboat and christened it *Millie*, after their beloved dog.

For the rest of the population it was a place to eke out a hardscrabble living, usually doing one or more service jobs such as landscaping, restaurant help, or driving taxis. They serviced the people who flew to Miami to escape the harsh winter of the north and the wealthy people who made it their own private playground. The people in this group were mainly poor blacks and Hispanics who earned so little that they were actually eligible for welfare.

Carlos lived in the Little Havana section of Miami that was predominately first- and second-generation Cubans who fled when Fidel Castro came to power. His father worked as a busboy at the Flamingo Hotel on Miami Beach for forty years before retiring with a small going-away party, a white cake but no gold watch.

Carlos was employed as a landscaper for Miami Tropical Landscaping, a company owned by Anglos but that employed thirty-two Hispanics and blacks to do the backbreaking work of trimming the numerous palmetto and palm trees that grew on their clients' oceanfront properties.

Since the austerity measures were implemented, service jobs all but disappeared, along with the meager salaries they paid. The rich sought refuge and safety in their oceanfront mansions. Initially this social arrangement lasted without challenge, but as the poor could no longer feed their children, their anger grew into a murderous rage as they listened to their children cry at night of empty stomachs. It didn't take long for the poor to determine where all the money and food was located. The rich of course had taken the precaution of hiring armed guards—really no more than violent thugs—to keep the poor away.

Miami's city streets turned into a bloody violent civil war. While the rich had the guards willing to use their guns, the poor had the masses and the righteous anger of the hungry. Mobs of the less fortunate stormed the mansions, and while many were killed, they were able by sheer numbers to overcome the guards and vent their long-simmering hatred toward the wealthy who time and time again fought against giving them a living wage and treated them with disrespect.

As the violence escalated, Maryann and Jack knew it was time to go. They packed all the food and fresh water the boat could hold, a few personal possessions they couldn't bear to leave behind and, of course, Millie, and set sail out to sea. The boat caught a breeze and sailed two miles off the coast before Jack set anchor. Jack and Maryann were on their boat having a simple lunch when the Chinese set off the NEMP attack on America. The effect on Miami was instantaneous. Blocks of homes caught fire, and without fire trucks or firemen to fight it, it spread like an inferno. Chemical plants exploded, spewing their deadly poisons into the air. They watched in horror as an American Airlines commercial plane, devoid now of all its electronics due to the blast, tumbled from the sky, crashing into the Atlantic Ocean, most likely killing everyone on board. What they couldn't see or hear was a young woman grasping her father and whispering, "I love you, Lawrence," as the plane went down.

No words could describe how they felt. They sat in silence, holding each other's hands, watching as their adopted city burned. Jack joked that they could live off the fish he caught, and Maryann said they'd starve.

After sitting in the quiet, knowing that this could be their last moments together on this earth, Jack eventually went down below and brought up a vintage bottle of Robert Mondavi Private Selection Merlot, his wife's favorite. Jack opened the bottle and poured two glasses. They had just taken their first sips when they saw the missile launched by a Chinese sub just off the coast come out of the ocean and fly into the sky above Miami. They instinctively knew what it was and what it meant. They hugged each other tightly, looking only into each other's eyes, mouthing the words "I love you" and holding Millie on their laps as the Chinese nuclear bomb exploded.

Carlos, his loving wife, Juanita, and their five small children were eating a modest dinner of rice and beans when the nuke detonated.

After that, nothing. Almost all of Miami and its population was instantly vaporized in the intense white heat of the explosion. The ones who weren't would wish they had been. The blast caused a tsunami that raced ashore and destroyed the nearest twenty blocks of homes, drowning any who survived the nuclear blast.

The class divide between the poor and the rich was eliminated in one brief, horrifying explosion.

In San Diego, as in Miami, chaos reigned. Hunger and fear prevailed. The population—one that historically consisted of military families and their influences—looked to the San Diego Naval Base for some hope of civility. On this day, there had been an announcement of a fresh water supply plus some ration distribution. Thousands swarmed for both the free water and the perception of being safe by being so close to one of the most powerful navy bases in the world. Little did they know that the NEMP attack had rendered the large aircraft carrier, and the two battleships in port, useless. The base's early warning detection system was made inoperable, and no warning would be coming from NORAD. The sailors scrambled to their assigned posts while their commanders waited for orders that would never come.

When the Chinese nuclear bomb was launched from beneath the ocean and traveled into the air above the naval base, the sailors, men, women, and children watched helplessly as the second bomb detonated, annihilating everyone.

China made good on its threats.

WASHINGTON DC

7 p.m.

PROMPTLY AT SEVEN, as promised, the Chinese delegation turned onto Pennsylvania Avenue. They arrived in three military jeeps flying the Chinese red flag. They were waved through security and escorted by a team of marines up the elevator and into the Oval Office in the West Wing. The president watched them as they silently took their seats in front of his desk, the last president who would ever sit there. His Cabinet stood stoically behind him. They had already received the preliminary reports via a Chinese courier who brought them video evidence of two nuclear detonations. One in Miami, the other in San Diego. The reports indicated both cities were destroyed, with massive loss of lives.

"Mr. President," the head of the delegation said, pulling a binder out of his briefcase, "You need to sign these documents now, please. I was told to inform you that unless you sign them immediately, and I notify our authorities that you have done so, we will resume our nuclear attack on your country. As you can see, this form shows that you have unconditionally surrendered the United States and all of its land and assets to the People's Republic of China.

Also you will find a list summarizing the information and documents we need from you. Do this now, please."

President Mann reviewed the documents that lay before him. He had never seen an unconditional surrender form before, but mused that there were many such documents signed in history. Before today the only one ever signed in the United States was when General Lee surrendered the South to General Grant of the Union Army. Now he was surrendering the United States to China. He felt physically sick to his stomach.

He picked up his pen and, with an angry flourish, signed his name to the documents. The deed was done.

America was no more.

Winter, 2025

AMERICA

THE CHINESE QUICKLY set up their own communications on private channels using Chinese satellites not accessible to Americans. They commandeered the airports, harbors, and train stations, and began to rebuild America with Chinese technology. They forced Americans into hard labor and executed hundreds of thousands.

In the coming weeks, hundreds of Chinese troop ships and cargo planes began landing at sea and land ports throughout the United States carrying thousands of Chinese soldiers, tanks, jeeps, and trucks. More thousands, much to the surprise of the United States, came over the border from Mexico, where they had been waiting all along. The US military was under orders to surrender their weapons to the Chinese, and for the most part they did. American soldiers are well trained in following the chain of command, and when their superior officer told them to relinquish their weapons, they complied. Truth be told, most just wanted to get home to their families. The few soldiers who took it upon themselves to fight on found that they were severely outnumbered, and did not have the resources or the manpower to resist for long. For those few who did resist, the Chinese decided to make a public showing of what was to happen to anyone who made that choice. Those resisters who weren't killed in the brief skirmishes were brought to public squares in chains, where they languished in the elements until the Chinese put them to death by crucifixion. The deaths were painful and sent a powerful message to anyone who may have thought of further resistance. Their families were incarcerated in labor camps, which was essentially a prolonged death sentence.

The first large detention centers were established in the former military bases, on college campuses, and in the cities. Where there were none, makeshift camps were built, surrounded by razor wire and guards with orders to shoot on sight anyone attempting to escape. American citizens were ordered to report with photo identification, which the Chinese scanned into a computer and matched against their lists of all political and military leaders. When identified, these leaders would be quietly removed and shot. All others were herded into detention centers and given starvation rations with assigned work details. Any American caught outside the detention zones would be shot by soldiers stationed in the surrounding watchtowers. The true purpose of the detention centers was not to detain Americans, but to kill them. City dwellers offered the Chinese no usable skills they did not already possess. By putting them on starvation rations and assigning them to hard labor, they hoped to cut the population of Americans by 75 percent.

China needed America, not Americans.

The population living in rural areas were allowed to remain in their homes for the time being, providing they did not cause any trouble and continued to work in the fields. They were also required to turn in all firearms. These people would be needed to maintain America's vast wheat and corn fields; at least until more Chinese inhabited the farmlands, and then those Americans would be dispensable as well.

Due to America's liberal policy on gun ownership, there were an abundance of gun owners who either hunted or target shot. When the Chinese landed, there were hundreds of thousands of Americans with guns. All combined, it would comprise one of the largest standing armies of the world, and it had always been thought that this fact alone would protect America. But by destroying the communication infrastructure, these loyal patriots had no way to communicate with each other. Tom couldn't call Joe and say, "Get the men together and we'll meet at the park and form a plan." Joe and Tom were alone, and despite all the good intentions of wanting to protect their country, the fact remained that they were not trained soldiers and thus no match for the crack Chinese troops. After a while, they too laid down their weapons.

The world watched but did nothing.

AMERICA, 2025

WHEN THE CHINESE conquered America, the first edict issued by Xi Chang read that all religion was banished, and anyone practicing it would be dealt with severely. Churches were ordered shuttered immediately. He had his troops set fire to them, then bulldozed the charred remains into the ground. The only punishment for disobedience was execution, and the Chinese enforced it without exception or hesitation. At first, across the country, it was met with disbelief. The larger churches in the more populated cities were commanded to immediately close their doors and stop their services. When they did not comply, special Chinese execution squads would arrive without notice, usually on a Sunday catching parishioners at prayer. The carnage was terrible. No warnings were given. Anyone and everyone in church would be shot, and the structure burned to the ground with the people in it. The fact that some were still alive mattered not. After a few short, fearful months of that policy, church attendance dropped to almost zero. It took the Chinese longer to get to the smaller churches, but they were equally draconian in enforcement when they arrived.

The truth of the matter was that for the most part, Americans had been turning away from religion for some time now. Most polls taken before the Chinese invaded

US shores indicated people were spiritual, not religious. Attendance in churches was at an all-time low. Partially to blame was the Vatican itself. The Roman Catholic Church was hit with numerous scandals—not in the least were the burgeoning sex abuse cases involving young children which the church refused to acknowledge. Instead, it simply chose to pay off the victims. The offending priests were shuttled off to unsuspecting new parishes where they were free to sin again. In addition, the Vatican banking fraud scandal came to public light. Most practicing Catholics never knew that the Roman Catholic Church had its own bank which wasn't subject to any banking laws, domestic or abroad. The bank had some questionable lending practices over the years, to say the least.

When Pope John Peter was elected in 2018, he pledged to clean up the corruption. He launched an investigation into the church finances as a result of allegations of financial transactions with unsavory and immoral people with criminal backgrounds. He was hailed as the pope of the people. He rejected the trappings of the office; fired his chef, preferring to cook his own meals; and drove himself in a small Volvo, giving his security detail fits. Pope John Peter began to dig deep, pledging to bring light to the dark and secretive Papal Bank. He died mysteriously of unknown causes shortly afterwards. Many speculated that he was poisoned by one of his own. It was easy for Christians to think that if the Church could not follow its own doctrine, why should the average churchgoer do so?

November 2026

NORTHERN MAINE

THE SUN WAS beginning to appear low on the horizon, and the red sky promised another fine day. Lawrence went to every hammock, placing his hand over each man's mouth and shaking them awake. They operated in silence; a man shouting inadvertently when woken was a risk. The men quickly left their hammocks and folded them tightly, placing them into their backpacks while shaking the sleep out of their eyes, their dreams fading in the daylight. Lawrence expected the same strict discipline from his soldiers that he demanded from himself. Each man carried his rifle, six-inch knife with a serrated blade, ammo, fish hook and nylon line, an ax, and a machete. The knife, ax, and machete were always sharpened until they had a killing edge. Each man carried the Chinese QBZ-95 military assault weapon. Despite its odd name, it was one of the finest military rifles ever produced. They were also plentiful, as the men just took them from the Chinese they killed. It was lightweight and simple to operate. It was chambered for the 5.8 x 42 mm cartridge, held a standard clip of 30 rounds, was gas operated, and could fire 650 rounds per minute. You could mount either standard optical sights or a night vision scope. Underneath, it held both a grenade launcher and a combat knife bayonet, either of which Lawrence and his men could use efficiently. They had to operate by stealth. Get in, kill the Chinese, and disappear back into the forest. They took a perverse pleasure in shooting the Chinese with their own weapons.

When Lawrence fought in Afghanistan, he operated as a one-man killing team. His weapon of choice was a M40A1 sniper rifle, with a 10 power Unertl sniper scope. Sometimes he would be away from his company in a remote area controlled by hostiles for more than a month. They wouldn't know whether he was alive or dead until he came straggling back into camp. The Taliban called him the White Ghost, and feared him as much as they feared the enemy drone strikes. When they spoke of him, they did so in whispers, as if saying his name aloud would summon him like a demon from hell. His kills became legendary. No one was safe from the long reach of his rifle. He would always volunteer to take the missions deemed too dangerous or even suicidal, but he always made it back alive. At one point the Taliban put a large bounty on his head, but none of the enemy fighters were particularly motivated to seek him. They weren't in that much of a hurry to meet Allah, and the promise of seventy-two virgins wasn't motivation enough.

The men gathered around the campfire, each helping himself to a cup of steaming hot black coffee. Cream and sugar were a luxury from the past, and Lawrence insisted that even if available, they were not to be used. His men were hard and pissed off, and he needed to keep them that way. They boiled coffee beans, crushed by the handles of their knives in a metal coffee pot without a strainer. If left alone long enough, the grinds would sink to the bottom of the pot, or so was the thinking. Most just endured the bitter brew, feeding on it. Dried game, usually venison, accompanied by a piece of hard bread and cheese, sometimes moldy, made their morning meal.

Lawrence spread out his topographical map of the area on the forest floor. He pointed to their current location, which was due south of the US-Canadian border in the woods near St. David on the American side. He traced a route with his finger where they would travel along the St. John River, now frozen over with thick ice, to the Canadian border town of Madawaska. The Chinese had set up a border crossing station and used it as an operational post. Their job, Lawrence told his men, was to take it out with extreme prejudice. Like every other mission.

"We'll follow the river until it makes the bend into Madawaska, and then skirt the thick cover of the wood line until we reach this grove of pine trees. We'll wait there until dark, and then hit them hard and fast. No prisoners, no survivors." He didn't have to tell them. "The border station is here, just three hundred feet north. They will have a fuel dump for their generators, and a communications building or shack. We take those out too. We can replenish supplies, and tail it out of there. As soon as the base doesn't report in, they'll be sending their Z-6 attack helicopters, and we want to be long gone. Not sure how many men they'll have, but it's a good guess more than we're used to, as this is one of their major border crossings, and they may be on the lookout for us."

He looked at his men in the early morning light and saw no fear in their eyes, just the iron determination in anticipation of the dangerous field assignment he had just given them. They knew the Chinese were aware of them and made their capture or death a high priority. Each of the men knew what their future held. Sooner or later, the Chinese would find them. They pushed this thought away from their minds, as it would only hasten their demise. Each of them had a personal reason for hating the Chinese, beyond the fall of America. To a man, they had lost loved ones, and now their only goal was to avenge those deaths and kill as many of the hated Chinese as they could. Lawrence taught them to harness all of their emotions into a cold, murderous rage directed at the Chinese. The fear of death never entered their minds or hearts, or sympathy for the men they killed. Lawrence and his men were being swept along in a swift current that would ultimately carry them to their deaths. They could only hope for a quick one, not wanting to be taken alive. If they could alter their fate, disappear off into the woods, they wouldn't.

Usually, he and his men would sleep hidden deep on the forest floor by day, and run operations using their night vision goggles after dark. The Chinese were well trained and disciplined, so Lawrence always cautioned his men not to underestimate them, but the human body naturally relaxed when the sun went down. Being alert night after night, it was only natural for them to relax some, even knowing how this dangerous complacency could get them killed.

The men broke camp silently, carefully removing all traces that they had been there. They checked their weapons, ran their fingers along the blades of their knives, and followed Lawrence deeper into the woods. They hiked for the better part of the day, stopping only once to sip water and check their bearings. When they were on a mission, Lawrence did not allow them to eat anything but a small snack, as he wanted them alert, and a hungry man is an alert man.

Lawrence knew that a great part of what kept him and his men alive was that they were closely in tune to each of their five senses. Beside sight and sound, he honed their senses of smell, touch, and taste. They learned to pick up the scent of the tobacco the Chinese smoked, the smell of green tea being brewed a hundred yards away, and knew by the taste of leftover rice how long ago the Chinese had left an area. Lawrence and his men were not the only hunters in the woods. Roving killing squads of Chinese soldiers, with orders to shoot on sight, were always on the hunt for any remaining militia groups still active. So Lawrence did not limit disguise and deception to just defense, but as a center-piece of offensive strategies. Their lives depended on it.

The sun was just beginning to set as the men reached the hostile outpost, throwing long shadows through the pine trees that towered over two hundred feet in the sky, giving the men another layer of camouflage. Lawrence took out his field glasses and scoped the border checkpoint. He could see two Chinese soldiers manning the barrier that stood between the United States and Canada, though he had to remind himself it was all Chinese territory now. A lantern was lit inside the shack that bordered the gate, white smoke entrails coming out of the flue on the near side. He could see no other buildings that could house additional soldiers. Two twin one-thousand-gallon diesel fuel storage tanks were safely located fifty yards from the shack. It was quiet. If it was a trap, it was a good one.

Lawrence raised his hand and waved two fingers to the east side of the checkpoint. Two of his men silently moved in that direction, step over step, moving slowly, careful not to step on a dried stick and alert the guards. Silence, not speed, was the goal. They stopped while they still had cover, placing themselves in killing range. They each raised their rifles and held their sights on the center of the chests of the guards. Lawrence pointed his finger first to another man, then to the ground, to indicate he should stay there and keep a watch for any kind of movement he may have missed. With a nod of his head, he and the other man made their way to the guard shack. When they were within fifty feet of the shack, he broke cover and sprinted to the building. Simultaneously each of his first two men fired a single killing shot at the two outside Chinese guards. Both wordlessly fell to the ground dead, their faces registering surprise at the bullets that suddenly slammed into their chests. At that precise moment, Lawrence kicked in the door to the shocked faces of the three remaining Chinese soldiers. One ran to pick up the receiver of the shortwave radio. Lawrence raised his weapon and fired. The man's eyes jerked upwards as he fell noisily to the floor. The other two quickly raised their hands in surrender. While his man trained his rifle on them, Lawrence pulled the maps from the wall, stuffing them into his rucksack to be studied later. He then placed all the remaining papers in a pile to be burned. Giving a cursory look around, satisfied he had everything of value, he had his men bring the two remaining Chinese soldiers outside, and forced them to kneel in the dirt. He first asked them if they understood English. They spoke in hurried, pleading tones in which they no doubt were begging for their lives. Lawrence raised his rifle slowly to let them know what was coming.

"This is for Amy," he whispered as he pulled the trigger. Twice.

NORTHERN MAINE

THE BLASTS OF the Chinese NEMT bombs did not affect most of the heavily timbered region of northern rural Maine. The terrain, heavily blanketed with towering pine trees and mountains, took the brunt of the damage, dissipating much of the electrical impulses. Anything south of Bangor, though, was toast.

The townspeople knew what happened…bad news travels especially fast. They sought answers in their churches, from their family and friends, but details were sketchy. More news filtered out of small bait and tackle stores and coffee shops than the official news outlets, as television screens went blank and the phone lines were down. Most assumed it was a nuclear attack. Most figured it was the Chinese. Living in the north woods, where nor'easter blizzards would knock down power and phone lines, more than a few folks had the old-fashioned ham radios as a backup. This enabled communication with other ham radio operators around the country. The reports coming in were dire. The community drew around itself and its church, fearing the worst.

When Father O'Mallory heard of the Chinese edict forbidding religion and the abolishment of houses of worship, he met with his congregation that Sunday with solemn resolve. He told the members of his parish that he would not, could not, shutter his doors, and implored his parishioners not to attend Mass anymore. It was just too dangerous. Instead, they should pray to God in a more secure, secret location. The congregation listened to his words but held firm. They knew the danger, but they would worship God in the manner they had done for years. One day in the fall, when the leaves fell and blanketed the streets in hues of gold and crimson and the air began to chill, the Chinese came on a Sunday morning. The church was filled with parishioners' voices in song worshipping God. Soldiers surrounded the church, bearing machine guns and blocking all the exits. In panic some tried running but were mercilessly gunned down along with anyone else trying to escape. The captain of the Chinese unit went into the house of God and walked up the center aisle, where Father O'Mallory stood. "Renounce God now, or be killed," the captain ordered. The beloved priest looked out at God's beauty for one last time as the sun streamed in through the stained glass window. Turning to the captain without a trace of fear on his face, he said he would pray for the captain's and his soldiers' souls. The captain raised his pistol and shot Father O'Mallory once in the head, instantly killing him. Then he motioned to his troops, and they began to fire their machine guns into the crowded pews. Screams of pain and cries of anguish filled the small church that once knew only peace and love. Fathers and mothers threw themselves on their children, begging and pleading for their children's lives. It mattered not. The sounds of spent brass shell casings made an unholy noise as they clattered onto the church's wooden floor. When the screams ceased, the Chinese stopped their shooting and began to exit the church. This holy place that had once been filled with prayer and song was silent.

The parishioners were murdered in the house of the Lord.

The white clouds that filled the sky above the church suddenly turned black as the Chinese troops exited. Large hailstones the size of baseballs rained down from the sky. Windshields on the cars and trucks outside cracked and broke; lightning flashed to the ground, causing sporadic fires; and the hail turned into a torrential rain. It was if the heavens opened up in righteous anger.

The Chinese immediately ran to their military trucks, ducking the hailstones and the lightening. A Chinese soldier was hit by a flash of lightning and burst into flames, then another. A jeep carrying four panicked soldiers exploded into a fireball when it was hit by a lightning bolt. They quickly fled the area before burning down the church as per their orders. The commander would falsely report that the church was destroyed, and none of his soldiers would disagree. First, it was never a good idea to disagree with your commander; second, none of the soldiers ever wanted to go back to that church.

It was strictly by chance that Matt and his mother missed Mass that Sunday. They were ready to leave when their milk cow, Bessie, managed to get herself wrapped in the barbed wire that was strung up down by the creek. Matt needed to free her before he could think about going to church.

Bessie got herself tangled up pretty good, trying to reach through the fencing to get at the tender green shoots of grass that sprouted at the edge of the creek bed. While his mother held Bessie's head and calmed her down, Matt took the pliers, carefully cutting off the wire that was wrapped around Bessie's legs. Once that was accomplished, there were a few pretty deep cuts that needed attending. They led Bessie back to the barn, and with Mom still holding her, Matt cleaned out the wounds so they wouldn't fester, then generously slathered on an antibiotic ointment. By the time they got done, they knew Mass was long over.

"Matt," his mother said, "I'd still like you to take this apple pie down to Father O'Mallory. I promised him I'd bring it today when I came to Mass. I know he'll be looking for it. I'm just too tuckered out to bring it myself. And ask him to dinner sometime this week... make it Wednesday. Tell him I'll make his favorite... roast pork with stuffing and homemade applesauce. Okay?"

"Sure, Mom." So Matt stripped off his muddy clothes and jumped in the shower, hosing himself off. He put on a fresh white shirt and jeans and walked down the stairs and into the kitchen, where he put the still-warm pie under a clean red-and-white-checkered towel, and headed off for town.

He expected that after Mass the people would head home, but the cars were still there. Strange. The area was very still and very quiet. When he pulled into the church parking lot, his mind couldn't quite make sense of what his eyes were seeing. There were still cars and pickup trucks in the lot, but most of the windshields were broken. Some were on fire. There was broken glass on the front steps, and the front door was hanging by one hinge. All of his senses screamed at him that something was dreadfully wrong. It was then he noticed the Chinese jeeps. Next to them, some Chinese soldiers were dead on the ground. He mounted the steps and pulled open the broken door. It was the smell that he first noticed. The smell of blood was unmistakable, and he had smelled enough of it when he was a medic in the war.

He gagged, covering his nose and mouth with his hand-kerchief. The carnage was terrible. Bodies were lying on top of one another, parents lying this way and that, covering their slain children. Some of the people he recognized as his neighbors, others with their faces too torn up to identify. The smell of blood permeated the church and was splashed in random patterns against the pews and walls. The stained glass windows, for which the congregation raised the funds by holding bake sales, were now shattered in pieces. The different colored glasses littered the floor. Matt's eyes went to the altar and he could see the large body of Father O'Mallory, lying on his stomach, splayed across the altar steps. He walked quietly to him and turned him over, cradling his head in his arms and hands. He could see the gaping bullet hole in his head and the ugly wound it left. His eyes were still open but unseeing. He gently closed his lifeless eyes for one last time, made the sign of the cross, and asked God to accept this good man into the kingdom of heaven. He gently laid him back down on the wooden steps and heard a low moan. He stepped over the bodies to where the sound originated from, and saw that Nicky Clark was still alive, but bleeding. Nicky was sixteen, the son of the owner of the True Value Hardware store in town. Matt ripped open his shirt, probably the only nice one that he saved to wear to church every week, looking for where he had been shot. Nicky moaned in pain as Matt's fingers explored, then located the wound. He had been shot, but it looked like the bullet went cleanly through his right side. Nicky was in shock, so Matt picked him up and carried him to the basin of holy water that was in the brass bowl that stood in the front of the church. Taking a piece of his handker-chief, he wet the cloth and wiped the blood off the wound.

Nicky's eyes suddenly opened wide, and his hands latched on to Matt.

"It's okay, Nicky. It's okay. What happened?" Matt asked, looking around for any other signs that someone else might be alive.

"It was the Chinese. They just walked in and shot Father O'Mallory, then all hell broke loose. They just started shooting at everyone! My mother…my father…" he wailed.

Hell had broken loose, Matt thought, and the devil walked the earth. How else could you explain this sacrilege in the house of the Lord? "I'll check, Nicky, but you lie still. How long ago did the Chinese leave?"

"I…I don't know. Hours ago, I guess."

Matt laid Nicky's head down, being careful to keep it elevated, and told him not to move. He had lost some blood, but he figured he should be okay. Matt moved slowly among the bodies, carefully moving them apart. Most of the townspeople were here. He knew some of the men had gone off deer hunting yesterday, as it was opening day in Maine and they were eager to fill their freezers before the winter blew in. This was usually the only Sunday during the year folks missed Mass with Father O'Mallory's blessing. He found Nicky's mother and father in one of the front pews and could see that they were dead. His father had numerous bullet holes in his back as a result of his attempt to shield his family. He checked the other bodies, careful to see if anyone else was alive. They weren't.

Matt walked back outside to Nicky, picked him up, and carried him out to his truck, laying him down across the front seat. How could God allow this in His own house? As he closed the truck door, a dented black pickup truck with oversized tires slid into the lot. Matt ran out and grabbed George Comeau as he headed to the church.

"No, George, you don't want to go in there."

"Where's Abby?" he asked, his voice rising in panic. "I know what happened! I'm going to kill every one of those cowards!" George was a native Maine farm boy...big and strong. In his college days he had played offensive tackle for the University of Maine's Black Bears and had a clear path to the NFL. His dream of playing for the New England Patriots was dashed while playing against Amherst his senior year. He ripped a ligament in his right knee tackling the running back and was carted off the field in a stretcher. He ended up having two surgeries, but they couldn't completely repair the damage, so no pro team would take a chance on him now. Matt always gave George credit as he never wallowed in self-pity. He would say that God just had other plans for him, and he joked he probably would have gotten drafted by some crummy team like the New York Jets anyway. So he put his glory days behind him with a shrug and moved on with his life. Now, like most people who lived in the north woods, he did a few jobs to get by. He ran a lumbering operation for most of the year, and then in the fall he guided hunters seeking the elusive black bear.

"Is she in there?" he asked, his voice cracking with emotion.

He was talking about Abby, his high school sweetheart and wife of two years. "I don't know, George. I don't know" George walked into the church, hesitant, fearful of what he might find. Matt heard a loud wail come from within the church. A moment later George appeared, carrying Abby gently in his arms, her black hair flowing lifelessly toward the ground. "I'm going to kill every one of those heathens! I swear to God!"

"I think God has seen enough killing, George. Let's put her down and lay her to rest. I know the hatred you have in your heart right now, but we need to worry about them coming back and finishing the job. I have a wounded kid in my truck, and God knows how many people were not in that church. We have to round up everyone quickly and get out of here. The Chinese know we're here now, and they know we've broken their law, so I don't know why they left, but you know they'll be back. They left some of their dead out front. So you go get your backhoe, and I'll bring the rest of the bodies out of the church, and we'll give them a proper burial. It's what Abby would have wanted. When I'm done, I need to go home and tell Mom, and we both need to round up every person left standing. We can meet here at the church at five o'clock. We need to hurry."

"Okay, Matt." George carried his wife tucked in his arms, as if she might still awaken, to the cemetery behind the church, laying her body gently on the grass. He smoothed her crumpled dress and her blood-soaked hair, gently caressing her face. Not bothering to fight back the tears that fell freely, he whispered something to her softly, then tore himself away and drove off in his truck to get his backhoe and hunting rifle. The rifle first.

Matt continued to carry the bodies out of the church and lay them side by side on the hallowed ground. By the time he was done, George had come back with a small group of neighbors accompanying him. George took his backhoe and, in an untouched corner of the cemetery, dug a wide grave. With great sorrow and anguish, cursing threats against the men who did this, they respectfully laid all the bodies down in it. They put the body of Father

O'Mallory at the head, the shepherd still watching over his flock. George slowly covered the bodies with dirt.

"Matt, will you say a few words?" someone asked. "Something should be said."

"Dear Lord, please take the souls of these good people, wrongfully taken from Your Earth, into Your kingdom. Bless them and hold them tight to Your bosom, until we are able to join them again in Your kingdom in heaven. Amen."

A few of the men helped George as they smoothed over the dirt that covered the bodies. Someone placed flowers on the mass grave. Others stood around, not sure what to say or do. When they finished, Matt called them together.

"Okay. I know you seek vengeance, but that belongs to God, not you. What we need to be concerned with now is that we *must* leave town. We are no longer safe here. The Chinese will come back, and when they do, it'll be to finish the job."

"Let them come," George said, raising his rifle. "We have enough men and women to defend ourselves. This is our home!" A few of the remaining men clutching their own rifles yelled their assent.

"I know what you're feeling, George. We all do. But we are no match for the Chinese soldiers. This time they'll probably come with armed helicopters. Do you really want to see these people killed?" Matt asked as his eyes swept across the group of people before him.

"What can we do, Matt?" someone asked.

Matt had become a deacon in the church years ago. He decided that becoming a priest was not his calling, but he still wanted to serve both God and the people in his community. So he studied and became a deacon with Father O'Mallory's blessing, assuming some of the duties of the church. He was a respected member and regarded as a friend to all in town. He now became the de facto leader of the surviving townspeople, both religious and otherwise.

"We can't stay here. That's for certain. We need to get out of sight and hole up somewhere. Then, when we're safe, we can figure out what to do. First, let's organize into groups that have specific tasks. George, you take four men and go into all the stores and get every bit of survival equipment you can. Not just necessarily guns. I'm talking about cold weather camping gear, boots, socks, fishing equipment, lanterns, sleeping bags, knives, ropes, tarps, binoculars, freeze-dried food, and propane stoves, and as much propane and lantern fuel as you can carry. We only have one shot here, guys. We're not coming back. Better grab two or three canoes, paddles, and life vests. We'll need as much medical equipment and supplies as we can find. We're on our own medically speaking—there'll be no hospitals. Don't go crazy with the guns, but get as many long rifle 22s and bullets as you can get your hands on. It'll be the 22s that will feed us, not the bigger calibers, but get a few of those as well for deer. Bottom line, this is our only opportunity to stock up. After today, it won't be safe to return."

"Where are we going, Matt?" a woman asked.

"We'll head to a spot I know where my dad took me as a boy. It's very remote, but we can get close to it by truck. Then we'll have to hoof all the supplies in, but there'll be fresh water, and if the forest is dense enough, the Chinese won't see us by air. After a week, with this weather, our trail will be impossible to follow."

"What if the Chinese come back and follow the trail?" someone asked.

"Then we're in God's hands," Matt answered.

"Then we'll shoot as many Chinese as we can," George sneered, his heart screaming with rage and pain.

"No! We won't!" Matt barked. "The killing stops now. Only God has the right to take a life, and if any of you don't agree, then you can stay here and wait for the Chinese. I'm sure they'll be back and glad to oblige you, and then you can kill each other."

The group looked around, searching each other's faces, full of confusion and questions. "Okay, Matt," George said, nodding to the group. "We have women and children here. They need to be safe. Anyone firing off their guns at the Chinese will just get us all killed. Matt's right."

"Okay then. Mary, you get some of the ladies and go house to house getting warm clothes, especially for the kids. Put them in large trash bags. Grab some kitchen pots and pans, some knives, forks...well, you know. Anything and everything you think we could use. If you're not sure, grab it anyway. Make piles in front of every house, and the men can come by in their trucks and load it. Take whatever medicines you have. Think, people! Focus and think! Our lives depend on it! It's a clear night. We work until dark, and then in the morning we load up and hit the back roads. Fill all the vehicles with gas and any spare gas cans, but don't forget the matches and candles."

"Matt felt that he was all over the place, too many thoughts exploding in his head at the same time. He looked around and said to no one in particular, "God will take care of us."

THE NEXT MORNING

ONE THING YOU can say about people who live and work in the country—they know how to put their back into it to get things done.

Matt looked around at the group of people assembled near their vehicles, which were now loaded to the gills with supplies. He could see that some of the children brought toys, and that was okay. With their lives uprooted so violently, they needed these childhood items of comfort. Some brought pictures and photographs, one brought a rather ugly paint-by-numbers oil of Elvis that had been done by his wife, who was killed in the attack at the church. While some of the items seemed impractical, it also told Matt that they took his warning of the possibility of not ever being able to return home again seriously. They could lug the stuff.

He counted eleven men including himself, fourteen woman, and a few who were seniors like his mom, and eighteen kids of different ages. "God is with us, and He will protect us. But just as He doesn't put the worm in the bird's mouth, it's up to us to take care of each other. We are going deep into the woods...not a strange place for any of us. We grew up here, hunting, fishing, and camping. We know how to survive. God filled the forest with plenty of game and fish to eat. Wood to burn for warmth. Water to drink. I don't know why God chose us or this path, but He is with us. Father O'Mallory always told us that God is everywhere—not just in our church, where we paid homage to Him, but in every tree and under each rock. "

"George, I will lead our caravan to our new home. I want you to take up the rear so we don't lose anyone, and also keep an eye out for anyone who might be following us."

"Matt?" a woman called to him. "I brought every last bit of coffee grounds I could find!"

"See!" Matt laughed, providing a much-needed bit of humor. "God truly does provide!"

With that, Matt slid in his old red Ford pickup truck and drove out of the church's parking lot. He glanced once more at the church, the grave of his father and now his neighbors, and turned away, never to return.

TREK INTO THE WILDERNESS

L IKE MOSES LEADING his tribe out of Egypt, Matt would lead a group of forty-plus souls of men, women, and children into the deep wilderness of Maine.

They would drive northeast out of the last town in northern Maine and follow an old logging road called the Telos Road, a dirt road full of ruts and blow downs, going no more than fifteen miles an hour. Any faster and they would risk breaking an axle. It was only fifty or so miles until they would come to the Ripogenus Dam—or the Rip Dam, as the locals called it—which until bankruptcy had belonged to the Great Northern Lumber Company. It stood at the mouth of a rock walled canyon of the great Chesuncook Lake and was used to provide hydroelectricity for the paper mills in Millinocket. When the paper mills closed, the dam, being so far out in the wilderness with no sizable towns nearby to service, stood dormant, like a large stone man with no place to go.

When they reached the dam, Matt called a halt to give everyone a chance to stretch their legs and go to the bathroom. He joined up with George and walked to the long-abandoned control building, now with its windows busted, and leaning slightly to the left. Grass had grown in the doorway as nature sought to reclaim what was rightfully hers.

"After we cross the Rip Dam, there won't be *anything* for five hundred miles," Matt said to George as they overlooked the dam. "What concerns me is that if the Chinese are determined to follow us, they only have to follow this road, and sooner or later, they'll find us."

"Then we need to blow the dam. It would flood the road going south, and then nothing could get through. The only thing is, Matt, if we do this, there is no going back. We just destroyed the only way in *or* out. Your call."

"George, ever since I was a boy, I knew I was in God's hands. I always believed in Him and trusted His judgment. I believe He has a plan for us and there's a reason we are here now and heading up this path. So let's put ourselves completely in God's hands and open the main valve on the dam and flood it."

Matt and George gathered everyone around and told them what they intended to do. As most of them were still shell shocked at the preceding events, no one said a word, trusting their judgment. Most feared the Chinese more than being stranded in the wilderness. They moved their caravan of trucks and cars loaded down with all their worldly possessions forward and up the road north of the dam where they would be safe from the flooding waters. Matt and George rode back down to the main control shack and found all the electrical automation rusted with disuse. Using a sledgehammer and a lot of sweat, they were finally able to manually open the main lock to the dam, letting the millions of gallons of water rush out, flooding Telos Road and the land below.

They stood side by side, silently watching the water rush forward, saying a final good-bye to the life that they knew was gone forever. George held back tears as he thought about his wife whom he would never hold again, the child they would never have. Matt stood silently beside him, not knowing how it must feel to lose a wife, and chose not to say inadequate words. They nodded to each other, got back into their trucks, and headed deeper into the woods.

WILDERNESS CAMP

MATT WALKED AROUND the camp pleased. The site they chose was within view of Gray Brook Mountain, next to Long Lake, which would give his "family" fresh water and fish, with the surrounding forest teeming with game for food. The thick overhead canopy of pine trees would provide security from any Chinese helicopter that might fly overhead. Unlike the deciduous trees that would shed their leaves in winter, the pine trees would give them protective cover year round. They carefully drove their trucks and cars into a thick, impenetrable grove where they could not be seen by air, taking the extra precaution of covering them with dirt and pine branches.

Using the canvas tarps taken from town, they built wall tents good enough to keep people dry for the time being. He charged some of the men with the task of cutting down trees and constructing more permanent structures. Both women and men were charged with the urgent task of gathering firewood for cooking and heat to get them through the severe Maine winter. He built a smoke house, and while game was still plentiful, began curing meat and fish they caught. As animals began to hibernate for the winter, hunting would become much more difficult. Fresh water, thank God, would not be a problem, although they would have to chop through the ice with axes to get at it. In this part of Maine, the ice could get eighteen inches thick and could begin to freeze in October. Once the shelters were taken care of, Matt built a structure large enough to house everyone. This would be their church and communal meeting house. It was an open-air building for now, with just a roof to keep off the rain and snow. He found four large pine trees, almost forming a perfect square, and ran a rope eight feet high around them, covering it with a blue nylon tarp. Ugly but effective. On one of the trees, he hand carved the Ten Commandments; on the others, a simple cross carved into the bark facing inward to remind everyone that Jesus had died to take away their sins. Here they would celebrate Mass, in addition to hosting community meetings and sharing meals together.

Blended families began to form, only naturally. Children were taken in and cared for, some to parents who had lost their own in the massacre. Some survivors who had lost their spouses began to seek the comfort they had once known. Matt abstained but was not judgmental to those who did not. It was a human condition to love and be loved. He believed he had taken a silent oath to God and remained alone. One woman, who had been a teacher in town, set up a schedule of classes for the children. While she would teach them English and math and such, some of the men would teach the boys and girls alike how to survive in the wilderness. Matt would hold Bible classes every Sunday after they celebrated Mass. He thought that ironically, they were returning to a natural order of life. Living off the land, taking care of each other, and worshipping God.

As Matt watched the men, women, and children that now comprised his family, a feeling came into his body and mind. It was a guiding light from God. He had always felt the hand of God on his shoulder, comforting him and advising him, showing him the way. He knew that his future and the future of his family were already written.

God looked over them, and they would be all right.

Fall 2028

NORTHERN MAINE

WATCHING THE CHINESE soldiers' brains splatter over the fallen leaves, a gruesome kaleidoscope of reds and pinks and whites, stirred no emotion in Lawrence. It brought no relief or satisfaction, nor did any of the hundreds he had previously executed. One of the Chinese was young, barely a man, his ill-fitting clothes hung loosely on him as he lay crumpled in the dirt. His eyes in death bulged wide in fear as red spittle dripped out of his mouth. A hundred more or a thousand more would not bring Lawrence closure. It was not something he sought. A million Chinese executed by his hand would not bring Amy back to him. So he kept his hatred stoked, feeding it as if it were a separate being alive within his chest, poking it, and feeling the acidic bile rise from his stomach and burn in his throat. It was how he kept the memory of Amy alive, fresh in his daily thoughts. He knew she wouldn't approve of his vengeful killing. She would rather he disappear into the wilderness to live out the rest of his life in peace; but he couldn't. Only his death would bring him closure and reunite him with Amy. He wrestled with his religious beliefs. How could a loving God so cruelly rip the only thing he cared about from him? Why was he not killed too? Was he being punished for the killings he had committed while being a soldier? Weren't the deaths of terrorists justified? How could He let the Chinese mass murder so many innocents? Hoping to be reunited with Amy in death was a thought he had to believe in. Kindness and compassion had to be left behind; it would get him and his men killed. He only hoped God could see whatever good was left in his heart, where he could see only blackness. This fiery burning ember of hate was what kept him alive and enabled him to get up in the morning. He knew his men were weary. Tired of being hunted, living like a pack of wild wolves in the forest. They were soldiers and had all suffered a great loss at the hands of the Chinese. Still patriots to a country that no longer existed. A self-serving government that weakened the United States so much that it had toppled without a fight. He and his men forged their mutual respect and friendship that often develops by soldiers facing death in combat side by side. Each knowing that their mission would end in death, sooner rather than later.

"Let's move," Lawrence told his men, "before we have company."

The men stripped the Chinese of ammo, packed the maps into rucksacks, and reloaded their weapons. One of the men went to the fuel storage tanks and opened the valve, spilling two thousand gallons of diesel fuel on the ground. An ancient thought of not polluting the environment surfaced. It seemed like a lifetime ago. Lawrence spread the topo map on the ground and indicated where he and his men would head next. They were dog-tired and needed a break. He knew there was an outpost of survivors from Maine holed up in a remote area of the Allagash. He had made contact with them before they knew that the Chinese could possibly be monitoring the shortwave radios they carried. Their leader, Matt, only using a type of reverse Morse code and only precisely at a certain time, could be contacted. It was a chance they all had to take, as it was imperative to stay in contact no matter what the risk. Lawrence decided they would travel there. Being with other people would be good for his men, since being in a constant state of vigilance took a toll, though for himself he couldn't care less. He was born and bred for combat. It was the only life he ever knew until he met Amy. Perhaps he would drop them off and head out on his own for a while. It would be good for his head not to have to worry about his men. He could travel faster by himself and do a reconnaissance on the outlying areas.

He indicated on the map where they would head, noting the steep and heavily forested terrain they would have to cross. His men nodded wearily. There were a series of fast-moving streams and rapids they would have to portage. The good news was they could be fairly certain the area was far enough and remote enough that they probably wouldn't come across any Chinese. He knew they were hunting him now—they had to be, with all the carnage they left in their wake. At one of the last outposts they hit, one of the Chinese spoke enough English to let them know that they were known as the ghost soldiers, legendary as the witch in the woods. After Lawrence interrogated them, he left the dead bodies to let the Chinese know they were there. Sending the message…you're not safe.

The men followed Lawrence single file into the forest, quietly stepping on wet brown pine needles, following a deer trail that led away from the Chinese outpost and southwest into the dark woods. Where some feared the unknown of the forest—the nighttime sounds, the unknown dangers coming from the black, brown, and green shadows—Lawrence always felt it was where he belonged. Alone, away from the mindless chatter of civilization. They picked their way through the heavy brush, following the natural terrain silently, placing one foot in front of another, heads peering around for any shape that might not look natural or any metallic sound or smell that would indicate the presence of man. They communicated with hand signals and set a brisk pace. They would stop and rest after they put many miles between them and the Chinese. It started to rain lightly, and the dark clouds heavy with moisture moving in from the east promised an even heavier rainstorm. Without breaking stride, the men grabbed their lightweight rain ponchos out from their backpacks and pulled them over their heads. The ground became soft with the rain, covering both footprints and sound. They hiked until the rain stopped. The late fall sun, a golden orb in the midday sky, turned the day sultry. The men stopped in a grove of trees, halfway up a hill that afforded them a clean line of sight front and back. They stripped off their ponchos and, for the first time that day, drank deeply from their canteens. The men sat down, spreading out. Safer that way. Lawrence walked the perimeter, breathing in the smell of pine needles and wet bark. Knowing the area was secure, he had his men take off their packs and get some shut eye. He would keep the first watch while they grabbed some well-needed rest. Measuring the light still remaining in the sky, he decided he would give them an hour off their feet before they continued on their journey. According to their location on the map, the American outpost might be a good two- to three-day hike. With no one behind them, they could slow down their pace and arrive there somewhat rested.

Lawrence pulled off his backpack and stretched out at the base of a large oak tree, looking backwards at the trail they just came up. He checked the action on his rifle, making sure he had a fresh cartridge in the chamber, and then placed it across his legs. His mind journeyed, drifting across the years. If someone had told him that the great America would fall without a shot being fired, he would have laughed. The policeman of the world toppled by a thug nation. He never considered himself what he would call a religious man. He had seen too much of mankind's violence inflicted on his fellow man not to have doubts, and was plagued with questions of faith over the years. He believed in God, tended to follow the Old Testament rather than the New one, liked the eye for an eye mentality, and believed God gave us the Bible as His guide for living a righteous life; however, he also believed in the old saying that in order for evil to succeed it only needed good men to do nothing. He never believed or said he was doing God's work while a soldier—he was far too humble—but he did have a strong sense of right and wrong. Indiscriminate killing of innocents could only be met with violence in kind. He had seen firsthand al Qaeda's butchering of women and children. Men tortured before being beheaded for no reason, women raped and stoned, children's hands cut off. No, diplomacy and threats of economic sanctions had no meaning for this kind of fanaticism. They only respected violence, and violence is what Lawrence brought them. Still he wondered why God allowed His children to act this way. He could only reason that good and evil was a choice. Right and wrong. God versus the devil. Amy convinced him to give up his battle, to turn in his uniform and come to America. Now here he was, back doing probably the only thing he was really good at. Killing. He hated the Chinese, not just for their war with America but also for their unnecessary, ruthless mass killings and enslavement of people. Lawrence understood war, the festering religious hatred, the envious greed. What he couldn't grasp was the intentional killing of people who were mere bystanders of history, with no compelling role in the drama of war. How on earth could you justify killing an innocent child? Did each man harbor a seed of evil deep inside, just awaiting the right circumstances for it to blossom into a hateful poison?

A squirrel scurried down the tree, shoving fallen brown acorns into its cheek, oblivious to the silent man near it. Its concern was singular: storing enough food to last it through the harsh and long New England winter. It reminded Lawrence that this part of northern Maine was still untouched by civilization and all of its woes. It still remained in a primal existence the way God created it. What would God have to say about this new world? More importantly, what would God do?

Fall 2028

NORTHERN WOODS

LUGGING HIS BROOK trout over his shoulder, Matt followed the winding trail along the shoreline of the lake through the trees that would lead back to camp. Despite the pine needles on the well-worn trail, he could feel each pebble and stone through the thin rubber soles of his boots. He wasn't sure what he would do once these wore out. Like some futuristic movie depicting mankind after a nuclear holocaust, there was no cobbler where he could take his boots to be repaired, or a Walmart where he could get a new pair of laces. Some of the men had taken green ferns from the forest floor and mixed them with the pitch from pine trees, stuffing them into the soles of their boots to fill the cracks. According to them it seemed to work pretty well. He whimsically wished there was a store where he could buy a new pair. He thought back to the time he went down to L. L. Bean with his dad and mom as a kid. It looked like a skyscraper and was the biggest store he had ever been to, with three floors and aisles and aisles of outdoor hunting, fishing, camping gear and clothing. His dad bought him a pair of rubber-soled hunting boots with tawny brown leather laced upper top, and a jar of mink oil to keep the leather soft and water-proof. Looking down at his feet, he now looked more like a beggar in some National Geographic magazine story. His boots, still wet with the mud from the shoreline, looked as though they could split and fall apart at any moment, his ankles stubbornly brown with dirt. Some of the younger men, even the girls, just went barefoot, their skin hardening like a natural form of leather. In the warmer weather the men went without shirts, their muscles hard and lean from living in the woods. Most wore their hair long, wild and unkempt, eschewing the offers of a haircut with rusty scissors. They were reverting back to a time and life none of them really knew. They were living with a consciousness above their normal way of life. Only a collective belief in God and an instilled respect for their elders kept them from sliding into chaos.

As Matt crossed a gently flowing creek of clear, cold water, the scent of venison cooking on a spit over the open fire wafted through the air. An older woman was taking great care to slowly rotate the spit, evenly cooking the meat. As he rounded the bend, he could see a few of the women stirring a big iron kettle, the outside blackened with soot, no doubt filled with this evening's dinner of stew. It was what they ate almost every night, as it was the most efficient way to keep a multitude of people fed. Over in the clearing, away from the trees, fish, rabbits, and haunches of meat were being cured on smoking racks above a wet fire fueled by green branches. Some of the children were running around half naked, screaming and throwing pine cones at one another. Some things will never change, thank God. A few of the men off to the side were in a heated discussion. One, Tom, a big-boned Maine farm boy, had been advocating joining one of the militias and striking back at the Chinese. Matt knew that he was swaying some of the younger boys who looked up to him, so he planned to address it after tonight's dinner.

It was the first real challenge to his authority in the group, and he knew people wondered how he would handle it. Normally every night the group would gather around the dinner table and partake in both prayer and storytelling. The youngest members couldn't get enough of the tales of how life was before the great collapse of America. Some of the elders just wanted to reminisce about the good times before the war. A few people, including Matt's mother, were charged with keeping a written journal as best they could, trying to keep track of dates, birthdays, and now, after some years living in the woods, deaths. While the births were both wondrous and strengthened the bonds of the community, the few deaths they had were equally difficult. One woman, only in her sixties, had taken sick and become bedridden. Without a doctor or hospital, no one was able to identify the cause of her illness. To ease her pain, she was given narcotics taken from the local pharmacy before they left town, but the years dissipated their potency, and frustration grew to anger as she suffered. When she passed, people gave thanks that now she was with God and her suffering had ended. Matt and George went to a clearing near the camp and dug the first grave of the newly christened cemetery. They wrapped the woman in a white sheet and gently placed her in the grave. The people stood silently, their thoughts no doubt wondering about what would happen if they too became sick. Matt gave the eulogy, remembering her life and her devotion to family, God, and friends. After placing wildflowers picked from the fields, they shoveled the dirt onto her body. One of the men carved a cross, and with his knife, put:

Michele Shaw

Age 67

Loved by all

Killed by the Chinese

Matt stepped out of the forest path and into the open area where people were gathered. He added his lone trout to the pile of food being smoked, taking a little ribbing from the ladies about his big catch. He walked over and took his traditional seat at the head of the communal table. It really only consisted of two large hand-hewn planks that had been cut from a fallen pine tree, planed smooth and cobbled together. Equally long matching benches were made and were placed on either side. While there was no formal dinner time or seating, when the food was cooked, most people took the same seat, with Matt at the head. His mother, now frail, sat on his right side. The cooking duties fell evenly amongst the men and women. Most ate sparingly, conscious of the long winter coming around the corner. One by one the others took their seats. Bowls of fish with flaky white meat in a stew, grilled rabbit meat with plates of forest greens, were passed around. Juices from berries served as the salad dressing. They drank from pitchers of cold water freshly pulled from the stream. Matt looked around the table at both the smiling and ever-concerned faces. When he said, "Let us pray," everyone grew silent and bowed their heads.

"God, thank You for the bounty we are about to receive, and thank You for Your love and safekeeping. We have placed ourselves in Your hands." Then he began to recite the Lord's Prayer:

Our Father, who art in heaven, Hallowed be thy name.

Thy Kingdom come,

Thy will be done in earth, As it is in heaven.

Give us this day our daily bread. And forgive us our trespasses,

As we forgive those that trespass against us. Lead us not into temptation,

But deliver us from evil. For thine is the kingdom, The power, and the glory, For ever and ever

Amen.

Softly everyone said amen.

The men started talking excitedly about the abundance of deer sign they had seen in the woods, and wanted to know how many they would need to kill to get them through the winter. One man walking with his wife had seen a large black bear on a distant ridge, and she joked it would make a nice fur coat. While this was normal dinnertime conversation, everyone knew the real topic tonight was Tom's pushing to leave the camp and go fight the Chinese.

Tom didn't waste any time to voice his views. They had just begun to eat when he blurted, "I know what you're going to say, Matt. Killing is wrong, and I can accept the fact you feel that way, but you have to understand that some people deserve to die. We should join in the fight against the Chinese. We can't let them get away with killing our families." He nervously pulled on his black scraggly beard and looked around the table for support. Some of the younger boys murmured their agreement. The air in the camp became heavy with tension, although the night began to blow a cool breeze through the pines. This dissention had been coming for some time. Matt knew some of the younger men just couldn't accept that this was their life. Rather than being grateful for escaping the Chinese and having an opportunity to live in peace, they were restless. Itching for action.

"Maybe so, Tom. Maybe so. But that's God's judgment...not yours, or mine, or anyone else's. You don't get to decide who lives or dies, and you sure don't have the right to take a human life. If you're looking for guidance...if you want to know what God asks of us..." Matt turned to point to the tree behind him, "I carved those sacred Ten Commandments when we arrived here for everyone to see. Now notice I said 'Commandments'...not wishes or suggestions. It clearly states 'thou shall not kill.' When we came here, we agreed together that we would not bow to the Chinese edict to abandon our faith. We all had bloodlust that day we lost our friends and families at the church. But we swore an oath to go deep into the woods and keep holy His Word. We forswore any acts of vengeance...and that still stands now."

"Other men in other groups have taken up arms and are fighting."

"Yes they are. And you can join them if you want. But Tom, you remind me of the bird that leaves its nest before it can fly and falls to its death. What have you to gain by sacrificing yourself? That's what will happen. You can't fight the whole Chinese army. You're apt to get not only yourself killed, but everyone here in this camp. It wasn't our bombs, planes, or warships that kept America safe all these years. It was our belief in God. This country was founded by Christian practices that were based solely on the Scriptures, not some new modern church traditions or civic customs. America went astray when we traded our Christian values for the glitter of golden greed."

"It wasn't just greed," an older woman sitting in the middle piped in. "We let the government change our way of life. Why, I remember every town had a nativity scene set up in front of their Town Hall come Christmas. Then some genius starts yelling about separation of church and state, and the next thing you know we weren't allowed to do it anymore. It was against the law! Whose law? Not mine! Not God's! Can you believe it?"

"Not just that," another added. "I can remember when we praised God in school when I was a child. They outlawed that too!"

"Then the Pledge of Allegiance. They did away with that! Because maybe it offended a ten-year-old! Since when do children make the rules in our country?"

"We weren't a democracy anymore, I'll tell you that!"

"It got so every outside religion could do what they wanted except us Christians, who *founded* this darn country!"

"Our politicians sold us out, those weak kneed..."

"And the ACLU! They cared about every minority's rights except us...the Christians!"

"I'll tell you what happened. Just like Egypt. The pharaoh disobeyed God, and Egypt was laid to waste! That's what happened to America!"

"It got so bad I would get dirty looks when I wore my crucifix into Portland!"

"If God sees fit to send this scourge upon us...

"Do you think we're being punished?"

"Well, God can keep us safe here..."

Matt straightened up from his chair and eased the cramping in his back. "I'll tell you what I think. I think Adam and Eve were thrown out of the Garden of Eden for disobeying God. Maybe God did punish America...I don't know. We certainly can't blame God for America's woes. We destroyed ourselves when we turned away from Him. Remember it was always 'One Nation Under God'? But this is our Garden of Eden now, and I believe we will remain safe here and protected by God's love as long as we follow His wish and remain true. God will give us our daily sustenance entirely from the land, its trees and lakes, just as He did for our forbearers."

Tom, sulking, got up and left the table.

"He'll be all right," Matt said, watching him leave. "Everyone here can understand what he's feeling. He lost people he loved too."

The sun began its slow descent, dipping below the pines and casting long, dark shadows across the camp. The camp's conversation turned lighter, about what young boy liked what young girl, and what new blueberry field was found in the forest. Matt observed that his mother was having a hard time getting around as she helped others to clear the table. He also noticed for the first time that her hair was completely white now and she stooped a little when she walked. He sadly thought she should be home on her farmer's porch with a hot cup of coffee, a blanket across her lap and a book in her hand. Instead she was living in an almost square cabin with another older woman. Matt had built it for them with nothing in it except two homemade beds, a small camp stove, and a makeshift desk with a well-worn Bible—not even a window to bring in the day's sunshine. None of the cabins had one, since you couldn't keep a cabin warm if you did. He would have to take a look at it and make sure it was buttoned up for the upcoming winter. For himself, Matt chose to live alone at the outskirts of the camp. He knew a few of the eligible single ladies favored him, but he grew to love his solitary existence and couldn't imagine sharing the silence with someone else.

Matt lingered at the table, enjoying the sweet smell of sap that was running from the wood someone had just freshly cut, the wood chips piled high nearby to be dried and saved for kindling. One of the men built a fire to ward off the nightly chill, the smoke drifting up in lazy rings and swirls into the sky. People began to sit around it, faces aglow in the light of the yellow flames, leaning forward warming their hands and feet against the upcoming night air. The sun drifted down, barely visible now, taking the waning warmth with it, as the others headed to their respective cabins.

Matt got up from his seat and, saying good night to the remaining people outside, began to walk back to his cabin. As he entered the edge of the trees, he slowed down to allow his eyes to adjust to the darkness. The sun was setting earlier, he noticed. He could feel his eyes burning and red-rimmed from lack of sleep. It came hard to him now. Maybe just another sign of getting old, he thought. Who would lead them when he passed? Certainly not Tom, he hoped. George would be his choice, if it was his to make. He walked on down the path until he reached his little one-room cabin. He twisted the little block of wood that kept the door shut, pulled it open, and lit the sole candle inside near his bed. It only gave a faint, flickering yellow light but was enough to chase away the nighttime shadows. He pulled from under the bed a small leather case that housed the portable ham radio, and opened it. Thank God it was one of the old models that had a hand crank to keep power to the batteries.

Knowing the Chinese were monitoring the airwaves, he kept in careful contact with the other groups with an infrequent irregular calling pattern. A modified reverse Morse code, and then only at precise times. Almost two years ago, when they did use the unaltered Morse code, a group that had been holed up in the northern region of New Hampshire went suddenly off the air. The prevailing thought was they had been infiltrated by the Chinese. Matt knew that Lawrence and his team went to the area to check it out and found that everyone had indeed been killed. He reported some disturbing signs of children being tortured to death in front of their parents, before they were killed as well. The site was as the Chinese left it, presumably to send a message to the remaining groups, as if they needed any additional message. Matt and Lawrence did not know how the rest of America was faring, except for the reports of wholesale genocide of Americans. Matt always regretted sharing this information with his family. There was no need. Their burden was already a heavy one, and filled with enough fear and uncertainty. How long before the Chinese found them, he now wondered.

Matt checked his watch; thank God it was one of the newer ones that had a lifetime battery. When the designated time arrived, he began a series of taps and clicks to signal Lawrence's group an "all clear." He sat on his bed and unlaced his boots, massaging his aching feet and pulling out the brush and twigs that still clung to his shirt and pant legs from the walk back through the woods. His socks were worn through at the toes and heels, blackened with dirt and grime from constant wear. They could only take so many washings in the lake. It didn't take long for a series of long and short beeps to confirm that Lawrence was still alive and was still planning to make his way to Matt and his family. Lawrence indicated it might take three or four days.

Matt did not tell everyone in the group apart from George about Lawrence and his band of soldiers. He knew that if Lawrence was captured or killed, the news would be devastating to the others. This would be the first time everyone met. When the New Hampshire family was massacred, it took Matt's people months to shed the day-to-day feeling that they would be next. Mothers wept silently, the men cursed the Chinese. But he would have to tell them now that Lawrence and his soldiers were on their way. They'd mostly likely have a heart attack if they saw a group of strange men make their way into camp—not to mention someone might shoot in panic. He always tried to allay their fears about being found. Matt reassured them time and time again that he had carved out a permanent enclave in one of the most remote and impenetrable tracts of wilderness in Maine, making it near impossible for the Chinese to detect. Or so he prayed.

After sending the signal to Lawrence, Matt shut off the radio and put it back into the brown cracked leather case, returning it to its rightful place beneath the bed. The radio had actually belonged to his father, who would use it on cold, clear winter nights more or less as a hobby. Now it was the only form of communication Matt had with the outside world. Thinking of his father scratched off the thin emotional scar that covered the painful memory. Matt was a full grown elder, yet he still missed his dad. His father's death was never emotionally resolved. His mother did better with it, but Matt took a long time learning to live without the physical presence of his father. For some reason, he never attained closure and never fully accepted his death. He was about to stretch out on his bed and blow out his candle when he heard his mother call his name outside the cabin door.

"Mother, what are you doing here?" he asked as he took a blanket and wrapped it around her while leading her to a seat on the bed.

"You looked so troubled, son, at dinner. I know you have a lot on your mind. Are you okay?"

"I am. I am. Sometimes... I just don't know. Mother, did you or Dad ever lose your faith. Even a little bit?"

"Matt, everyone does. Blind faith without questions... well, that's just plain dumb. Why do you think God gave us a brain and the ability *to* ask questions? That's what got those Arab terrorists so twisted. They just took it as gospel from their imams that it was okay to kill innocents. If they had thought for themselves, why then, how could they do it?"

"I know. But I mean you. When did you question your faith?"

"Matt, sometimes something happens that just strengthens your faith. Let me tell you a story you don't know. When your dad died, I was so angry—angry at God and at the world. With so many evil men in the world, I couldn't help but ask why God would take your father. I couldn't reconcile it, and Father O'Mallory could not say anything to give me comfort. Well, a few months later, you went to your friend John's house for the weekend. You boys were going fishing with his dad, and I was going to be alone and catch up on my reading."

"I remember..."

"Wait, now. It's my story. It was on a Saturday night. I remember it like it was yesterday. Raining like nobody's business. Every fool or critter had enough sense to be out of the rain. So here I am in bed, and I hear someone break into the house. I could hear them stumbling around in the kitchen. So I slip out of bed, grab your dad's shotgun, and quietly creep down the stairs in my socks. Well, there in my kitchen, silhouetted by the moonlight, I see a man with a kitchen knife. I raised the shotgun, aimed it right at him, all set to defend my home and shoot that bugger, when I threw on the kitchen light."

"I remember that, Mom. I had come home early from John's. Since we weren't going fishing, I thought I'd come home to help you. I was in the kitchen making a sandwich."

"Matt, if I hadn't turned on the kitchen switch and turned on the light, I would have killed my own son. Do you understand, son? God gives us the light to follow. The devil hides in the darkness. The devil would have had me kill my own son, but God had me look into the light, and here we are. Every day we have a choice of looking into the light or letting the darkness play with our insecurities and fears. That night, that awful night, whatever questions or doubts I had about Jesus or God left my heart. Matt, you're a good man, just like your father, and this is a terrible burden God has placed upon you, but He knows you can handle it. Can you stand one more story from your old mother?"

"Of course, Mom."

"A man is carrying a wooden cross and complains to God that it's just too heavy and he can't carry it anymore. So God tells him to go to this pile of crosses, hundreds of them, and pick another one. So the man puts his cross on the heap, and after much trying out different crosses, chooses one. 'Thank You, God, this is much better,' he says. Well, God says to the man, 'That is the exact same one I gave you. You picked the same cross.' You see, Matt, God never gives us a burden we can't handle."

With that, she lifted herself off Matt's bed, kissed him on the cheek, and let herself out the door.

Fall 2028

NORTHERN MAINE

HAVING RESTED BRIEFLY, Lawrence and his men were on the move again. The men's spirits were up knowing they were heading for Matt's camp, hoping that for the first time in ages they could rest their heads in deep sleep without having to take watch or worry about the Chinese appearing like bad demons in the night. There would, however, be no resting from the nightmares that still haunted them. There were no signs that the Chinese even knew where they were or were even pursuing them now, or at least that's what they had to tell themselves. They had been on rations for so long, eating sparingly, that Lawrence's promise of a bowl of rabbit stew sounded the likes of a sumptuous feast too good to be true. Their mouths watered involuntarily like a group of Pavlov's dogs hearing a bell.

They marched south by southwest following both the compass and the position of the sun. They crossed an open meadow, a sea of gold with thousands of sunflowers, fragrant scents blowing in the wind. The sky was barely visible with the heavy cloud cover, but the sun showed through in golden streams, brightening their mood even further. The woods were already bursting with fall colors, earlier here, driven by the colder northern temperatures.

When they reached the general vicinity of the settlement, rather than proceed directly into it, Lawrence had his men set a perimeter and then scaled the outcrop of rocks that overlooked it so he could first observe it through his binoculars. He left nothing to chance, and didn't want to lead his men into a trap. Complacency meant death, and maybe after three long years, death and the peace it brought would be welcomed. What he saw when he looked down onto the settlement was a ragged bunch of men and women moving slowly but with a determined purpose. Their faces were covered with smeared dirt and mud, whether to ward off the biting insects or just the result of living in the wild he did not know. They were stacking wood, cleaning deer, stretching hides between two white birch trees to dry, and sharpening tools with large, coarse files. Some older people were sitting down next to tattered clothes strung out on a rope to dry, lost in deep conversation. A man with dark brown eyes and a weather-beaten face was placing sharpened sticks outward around a small garden to protect its meager crop from the animal raiders of the forest. Despite its outward appearance of randomness, there was conformity as well. Ragged children, some naked, were kicking a partially deflated soccer ball, evidently being governed by a new set of rules. The settlement was comprised of no more than a dozen or so oddly shaped huts, built in various sizes and competency, staged around a larger building in the middle. Probably where they met for meals. This vista could have been as easily seen in a small village in remote Africa or India, or any third-world country. Aware it was established as a religious outpost, he still could see no posted guards, human or heavenly. A canoe bobbed in the current of the stream that ran by the settlement. Was this what was left of America? Bands of survivors hiding, cowering, waiting for death, be it natural or otherwise? Still a small laugh escaped his lips, as he was grateful to see other survivors. Satisfied there was no threat, he climbed carefully down the rocky incline, having come too far to take a careless slip and break his neck now, he thought with a grin.

The soccer ball skittered past the last hut, when its young pursuer came to a skidding halt. Here in front of the boy appeared five men with long, unkempt beards and bloodstained camouflaged clothes. The men stopped and smiled, putting up their hands in the universal language of surrender. They told the boy that it was all right, they were American soldiers and here to see Matt. The child, not waiting to hear anything else, turned and ran back into the village announcing the strangers. Men, women, and children quickly went out to meet them, having been forewarned of their arrival. It was the first time in years that the village had seen or spoken to anyone from the outside. For Lawrence and his men, it was the first time in years that they had seen someone they didn't have to kill. As they walked into the village, the younger men surrounded them and peppered the soldiers with questions of battles and Chinese killed. Some of the younger women smoothed their unkempt hair with their fingers and straightened the wrinkles in their skirts, giving the men their best smile, not having completely forgotten their flirtatious ways. The men still walked in single file until they reached the long wooden table and bench where a crowd awaited them. They were given cups of cold water, dried strips of jerky, and the promise of a feast in their honor later. Someone ran to fetch Matt, who was up on the roof of his cabin, laying an extra layer of pitch and mud to keep ahead of the snowfall. Lawrence looked around at the solemn remnant faces of God's faithful followers.

When Matt came into the village, Lawrence could recognize him immediately by the heavy mantle of responsibility he wore. The two men had not met but shared an unspoken kinship, two strangers set on a course of unavoidable destiny. They shook hands, and Matt introduced his family to the men.

"It's good to finally meet you, Lawrence. You and your men are welcome to stay as long as you'd like. In fact, why not just stay with us permanently?" Lawrence's men looked sideways at their leader. Their lust for battle and revenge had been worn down over the last few years. You kill enough, you kill part of your soul along with the enemy. Looking at the settlers, each man could envision giving up the fight, maybe living out the rest of their days in peace. Maybe even finding an available woman to love. A child to raise.

"Same here, Matt. The men and I appreciate your hospitality, but we'll rest up for a while then push on," he said, his face not looking for agreement with his soldiers.

"What have you heard from the outside world?" Matt asked, eager for news.

"China has completed its stranglehold on America. It's carrying out a widespread plan of genocide. Most Americans are in detention centers, given starvation rations, and being worked to death. There are rumors of mass executions of the elderly and young children. Ships of Chinese arrive almost daily. What I could glean from papers we captured from Chinese outposts, and whatever intel we've been able to piece together, is that America isn't the only country conquered. We were just the first to fall. Their game plan is to take over the world—they might have already—and once the US fell, no one could stop them."

"What happened to our Allies?"

"Allies? What Allies? As soon as we were hit, France immediately surrendered. Cowards the lot of them. How many boys died on the beaches of Normandy in WWII saving their country? They would have been speaking German if not for America. Others, in fairness, most of Europe, faced the choice of surrendering or annihilation. They had their own citizens to worry about. I hear the Aussies and the Kiwis are still standing, as is the Middle East. Believe it or not, Israel, Iran, and Iraq have joined forces against the Chinese. Years of diplomacy didn't work, but their common survival allied them. Go figure. They hope the Chinese won't nuke them since they want the oil in the region.

"Canada?"

"Canada has always had America to protect them, so they crumbled alongside us. The Chinese are quickly populating up there as well, since there are numerous resources such as timber and cattle. I did hear some stories of the Mounted Police not surrendering, waging a guerilla war like we are, but what can come of that?"

"All the more reason you should stay with us, Lawrence."

"My men can do what they please, but for me, I won't quit as long as I can take a breath."

"Revenge should be left in God's hands. Do you believe in God, Lawrence?"

"I don't know, Matt. I thought I did. But seeing what I've seen…sometimes when I am praying to God, it's like I'm praying to an entity I'm not sure I believe in anymore. Strange. Like praying to a stone carving or a passing cloud. Sometimes it's hard to believe in anything."

"God keeps His promises, Lawrence. His judgment is unavoidable, and heaven is open to all that believe in Jesus Christ."

"And what of the Chinese? When do they get punished?"

"God's punishment of evil is not on our timetable but His own. The Chinese unrepentant rebellion toward God *will* be destroyed and they *will* be thrown into the lake of fire, make no mistake. His judgment is final. Listen, you and your men are tired. We cleared out a supply hut and strung up some hammocks. Why don't you all get some well-deserved rest and we can talk over dinner."

"Thanks, Matt. We'll take you up on that. Is there anything we can do beforehand?"

"No, just get your butts to bed. Why don't you strip off those dirty clothes and I'll have them washed. We have extra clothing in a pile in the hut. I'm sure you can find something that fits. Grab something clean and get some shut-eye. We'll wake you if you're still sleeping."

Fall 2028

WASHINGTON DC

CHANG SAT ALONE in his office. Something shifted in his brain and a memory came into focus. He was a boy, a small child. His father had not gone into the fields that day, something which in itself was very unusual. He remembered his mother washing him in a small gray dented metal basin outside the door to their home, crying as she did so, having trouble even looking at him. He remembered other baths when his mother would always kiss him and stroke him as he squirmed in the soapy water, but not this time. She had reluctantly dried and dressed him, as if trying to hold on to this precious moment. He ate breakfast with his father at their small wooden table, his mother sitting beside them, crying and pleading with her husband not to go. Finally, the long walk into the village, passing other villagers who were unusually silent, their eyes lowered. The man and the small boy entered a room with a brown cracked desk within, where the local official sat on a chair that creaked when he moved. He could see a braying water buffalo outside the window and wanted to go to it, but he was still in the firm grasp of his father's hand. A man was standing still along the side wall, dressed in clothes Xi had never seen before. The green jacket was brightly colored with pieces of metal and cloth hanging down from his chest. A large, wide hat with two stern black eyes beneath it looked at him impassively. He was a bigger man than the others in the room; his father looked particularly small compared to him. Then his father walked to the man and, giving his son's hand to the stranger, turned and left the room with his shoulders heaving. Xi looked out the window, still seeing his father outside, now crying, untying the animal, leading it down the same path that they traveled to come here. His father never turned his head back to say good-bye.

Strange having that memory pop up like that, interrupting his thoughts. He hadn't thought of his biological parents in years. He knew some people made comments that they could never give up their children in any circumstance. Of course, these comments were never said aloud in Chang's presence. The truth was that he admired his father for doing what he needed to do to save the family. In a much broader stroke, wasn't that what Chang was doing for his Fatherland? The needs and good of the masses must always supersede the needs of the few—unlike the masses in America that wanted more and more without working, without sacrifice, while the weak-kneed politicians caved in to them for fear of being thrown out of their privileged lifestyles in government. No, that form of government has an end date, a time when it just runs out of money and can no longer support itself. Chang knew that sacrifice was the necessary foundation of change. This is why America needed to borrow tens of trillions from his country. He hated the Americans. They were given more than any other nation on the earth, yet it was not enough. A large land mass rich in natural resources, protected by an ocean on both coasts—it should have been the wealthiest nation on the planet, yet they spent money like a drunken sailor. It only took a stiff breeze to blow down the house of cards that America had become.

A knock on his door interrupted his thoughts.

"What is it?"

"Sir, that northern militia group has hit one of our border checkpoints again. This one occurred at the northeast tip of Maine."

"Survivors?" He expected none. The group always left a pile of dead soldiers behind, taunting him.

"No, sir, but a break. One of our recovery teams found a map left by the Americans. It may have fallen out and been left behind by mistake."

"Give it to me." Chang looked at the creased, folded topographical map. It showed the northern New England states, and parts of Canada. There were circles around all of his more remote outposts, and red lines through the ones that had been previously attacked. He knew this group operated in the area, but no matter how many traps he set, they always managed to elude him. He even stationed two attack helicopters in the region to respond immediately in the event that a distress signal could be launched. None ever was. He knew it was a small band, no more than five by the boot prints they left, but they were very evasive and deadly. Though they posed no tactical problem for him, he did not need the Americans to have a hero. So he committed more resources than he should have to the capture of these renegades before their legend grew. He even unsuccessfully tortured some former US military men to find out their identities, but to no avail. If he knew who they were, perhaps he could locate their families in the concentration camps to use as leverage; that is, if they were still living. American prisoners were dying off quickly. He desperately wanted to capture these men alive and have a most public death for them.

He studied the map, his anger rising at the number of his outposts that were terminated, and noticed a small pencil mark on the map in the north central part of the state. He pulled out another map in his desk and, comparing the two, noticed that the pencil mark was a few hundred miles, more or less, from a small town that his men had ambushed, killing some but not all of the inhabitants years ago. The troops had waited until Sunday and caught them together in church. The reports given to him were sketchy but indicated that some of them managed to escape into the woods. The same woods the pencil mark indicated. Could this perhaps be the base from which the rebels operated? Maybe or maybe not; but this was the first possible break he had, and he wasn't going to lose this opportunity.

He dismissed the man and called for General Lao Pengyou, an old friend and the head of his military division in the United States. His office was located downstairs in the old White House. When he arrived ten minutes later, Xi spread out the maps and showed the general what his analysis may have revealed.

"I want you to personally man a search-and-destroy mission in this area. I believe this is our best chance to eliminate these rebels, and if possible, I want as many captured alive as you can." Pointing to the map he continued, "I want you to block these small dirt roads, and the waterways here and here. You will have to use our WZ-10 helicopters, as the area is too remote for planes. You will have to drop in and approach by foot. Set your men in a large circle and tighten the noose until you have them. Commit as many resources as you need, but *don't lose them*. You will most likely find them along with some stragglers that got away from one of our previous attacks. Civilians are to be terminated on the spot. Everyone. No survivors this time. Remember, I want the militia unit taken alive and brought back to me. Do I make myself clear?"

"Yes, sir. I will personally handle the assault. If they are in the area, I will get them. I can't promise they will be alive, but I will tell my men that anyone who shoots to kill will themselves be shot."

"Very good. I want no communications getting out as a warning. This group has proven itself to be extremely resourceful and elusive. Select the best men you have, but run this as a silent op."

"I'll start on it immediately, sir."

"Excellent. No excuses."

With that, General Pengyou left the room and headed back to his office with both maps. It was a large area in which to run an assault, so uninhabited and wild he would need two battalions of men to ensure no one could sneak through the cordon. He would need no fewer than ten WZ-10 helicopters, fully armed and with a full complement of men. He made marks on the map at the best points to deploy his troops to quickly seal off the area. The waterways shouldn't be a problem, but he couldn't take a chance. Xi was implicitly clear about the importance of this mission, and he knew what would happen to him if he failed, no matter how many stars he carried on his shoulders.

He would not fail. The Americans were already dead. They just didn't know it yet.

The Camp

NORTHERN MAINE

Lawrence's men may have been dog-tired, but the smell of fresh rabbit stew and the hind quarter of a deer being roasted on a spit over an open flame outside their cabin dragged them from their deep slumber. Lawrence wasn't there with them. They knew him well enough to know he would be sleeping somewhere in the forest away from everyone else. You would think he would want the human interaction as much as they did, after the intense loneliness of being on a mission for so many years, but that just was not his nature.

The men swung their legs over the side of the hammocks, stopping to listening to the alien sounds of human conversation and laughter. Some children were outside peering in to watch these strange men who had slept fully clothed, their boots and rifles within their reach. It was heavy on each of the soldier's minds that it would be difficult to leave this peaceful place. They had endured hardships and deprivations that most could not know. They sat on the edge of their bunks, listening to a group of women within earshot sharing the cooking chores and talking about all the things they missed the most.

"Me? Give me a hot water tank so I could take a long hot shower."

"No, give me a nice steaming hot bubble bath."

"A hair dryer! Never in all my days did I think I would ever miss that silly little thing."

"Chocolate. Oh, God, what I'd give for a Hershey's chocolate bar."

"A nice glass of Chablis. Okay, maybe two—three glasses!"

"Hand lotion," said another, looking down at her chafed and cracked hands.

"Maybe a nice sexy dress," said another woman, glancing over at the soldiers.

"Yeah, right. To wear dancing?"

"Oh, honey, you don't need a fancy dress to catch their attention. Those poor boys look like they have been in the woods too long. A bear might start looking pretty good to them right about now."

With that, the women all laughed.

Lawrence appeared as an apparition out of the woods, rifle slung over his shoulder, the steely hard look in his eyes not diminished in the least by making it safely to the camp. If anything, he looked less at ease being in such an open place. He walked through the camp, nodding at whomever greeted him, eyes down, not wishing to join in conversation. He was not tempted nor longed for either the food or the women. For him, this was a temporary way station, a chance to let his men rest up before they continued on their path. He asked where he might find Matt and was taken by a young boy proudly toting a stick pretending it was a rifle. Looking at him, he felt momentarily sad as this child wouldn't be joining his local football or baseball team as he did at that age. Life was taken away from him by both the American politicians' weakness and the Chinese's lust for world domination.

He noticed Matt's hut was set fairly far away from everyone else's, something he would have done himself, had he lived here. The boy stopped fifty feet from Matt's hut and pointed. Lawrence ruffled his hair, and the boy, shouldering his stick rifle, turned around and went back the way he had come.

Matt was sitting outside on a stump of a pine tree that he had dragged up on his porch to be used as a stool. He was running a file over the head of an ax, sharpening it to a point where Lawrence could see the edge of the blade glisten in the waning sunlight.

"You would have made a good soldier, Matt."

Matt smiled wearily. "I was a soldier. CO. Four years. Spent time in the sandbox overseas."

"I had no idea. So you were a commanding officer. What division?"

"Conscientious objector. I refused to carry a gun. Got me six months in the brig, but I guess when they knew I was serious about 'thou shall not kill' they let me out to be a medic. They believed it was bad enough I wouldn't fight, then I ticked off some of the brass because I'd give medical aid to any soldier, ours or foe. I got by. Witnessed so many terrible things, makes you wonder how we can inflict such terror. There has to be a better way to solve differences than killing each other, maybe a nice game of poker."

"Good idea. If only it was that simple, huh? Well, the world as we know it is over. From what I hear the Chinese have a stranglehold on the planet."

"That Chinese greed..."

"Whoa there, fella. Chinese greed? What about the American greed? That's what got you here. You must know that. The Chinese just came in and picked up the broken pieces."

"No offense, Lawrence, but you're not from here. New Zealand is a long way away—besides, it's just a tiny island."

"Exactly. That's my point. I'm not from here, but let me tell you, growing up in New Zealand, America was the shining country to the rest of the world. It used to be held as an inspiration, the highest moral edifice for the rest of the nations to follow, but that all changed. Your politicians no longer served your country or its people, but themselves. As soon as they got elected into office, their only real concern was to get reelected and advance their own career. They had to 'get in line' with their own party, right or wrong. Their unbridled egos put themselves and their own political aspirations before service to their country. Integrity and honesty? That doesn't get you elected. Money does. They lined their pockets with hard working Americans' money. They answered to no one. They wrote the rules. Do you remember back some years when your two parties couldn't agree on a national budget, forcing the government to shut down for months? Did you know that Congress still got a paycheck while the men and women fighting for your country didn't? Listen, don't get me wrong. America *was* a great country. If it wasn't for America, most of Europe would be part of Germany right now. I'm just saying it was years of deficit spending, spending money you didn't have on social programs that hurt the American people by enabling them. The old adage…Give a man a fish and you feed him for the day, but teach him how to fish and you feed him for life."

"All true. But it wasn't just the politicians, Lawrence; it was a move away from God. Do you know America was founded as a Christian nation? We allowed religious freedom to all, but some liberal groups hijacked that freedom, pushing our own Christian beliefs to the side. The Christians became a minority in their own country. I remember when Sundays were always treated as a holy day. Mass followed by a home-cooked family dinner. We had blue laws preventing businesses from being open on the Sabbath, keeping His day holy, as it's said to do in the Bible. But businesses sued to open on Sundays—like you couldn't get your shopping done in six days? You don't think the owners of the stores worked on Sundays, do you? No. They made their employees do it, with the subtle threat of a loss of hours or even their jobs if they didn't. Then somehow we let school games take over, and that's all they were, games. Soccer games, football games, baseball games. Extra practices. Soon having a leisurely Sunday family dinner turned into grabbing a bite at the kitchen counter and running out the door. This is how we pay thanks to God? The one day, *one day* we were to dedicate to God, and we couldn't even do that. No, Lawrence. We turned our back on God, and He turned His back on us."

"I remember Amy telling me when she was growing up her parents refused to open their pizzeria on Sundays. They knew they were losing money, and everyone called them crazy, but they always said there were more important things." Looking around he continued, "So is this God's judgment? Is this how He repays His faithful? Seems like the Chinese are doing better than you guys."

"Do not speak lightly of God's judgment. I believe someday there will be a terrible reckoning. God gives us hope and inspiration at every turn in nature, Lawrence. If you listen carefully, you can hear the voice of God in a thousand different melodies that are sung to us every day in these woods surrounding us. Stay with us. Give up your fight and live out your days in peace."

"Peace? Waiting for the Chinese to come and enslave us? I'd rather die standing up than live my days on my knees. Besides, I'm not sure God wants me anymore. I've done terrible things..."

"We have all sinned in our lives, each one of us, many times. God forgives us; He only asks that we repent. Think about it. Now why don't we get our butts down to supper before your men eat all the food?"

The two men walked in silence through the woods, the smell of roasted venison guiding them. *Could I really be happy here?* Lawrence pondered. *Do I even know what God asks of me? I thought it was to wreak vengeance on those who would harm innocents. Now, it's all become one big blur. Could I really put down my rifle and lead a peaceful life? What about the Chinese? Surely they aren't going to forget about me.* Deep inside, he knew the inevitable consequence of his actions.

The men walked silently side by side into the main camp. One of Lawrence's men was chatting with an attractive woman, her hair more silver than grey, flowing down her back. They were leaning in close to each other, giving an air of intimacy, her laughing at something he said. When the soldier noticed Lawrence, he straightened up, with an undeserved guilty look on his face. Lawrence just nodded and walked past the couple. Another soldier was sitting on a bench with one of the settlers, taking apart a rifle, cleaning it, and working the action until it moved fluidly. Two of the other soldiers were kicking a ball in a pickup game of soccer with some of the kids. Lawrence felt a pang of guilt at the thought of taking his men away from this respite from the war. A war they couldn't possibly win. A war that would only bring about their deaths.

Matt and Lawrence made their way to the communal dinner table as food began to appear. Someone unseen rang a dinner bell, bringing the rest of the settlers and his soldiers to the table. The two men began to pick up the metal dinner plates that were set on the table, bringing them to where a haunch of deer roast was still being turned slowly over the now dying fire. While one man continued to turn the spit, another began to cut slices of the juicy red meat and place them on the individual metal plates. A small bookish woman, her hair tied in a loose ponytail, placed a bowl of fresh greens mixed with blackberries at the center of the table. Children filled the pitchers of water from the stream, walking around the table filling the blue speckled enamel cups. When everyone had their food in front of them, Matt began the prayer.

"Please bow your heads. Lord, thank You for the bounty of food we are about to eat. We thank You for Your eternal love and daily blessing. We especially thank You today for bring Lawrence and his friends to us safely, and ask that You keep them from harm and convince them through the Holy Ghost that they should remain with us and live in peace. Amen."

The group murmured "amen" together, and the conversation grew loud, the members eager to hear what the soldiers had seen. Previously Lawrence warned his men not to discuss operations, as these people were not soldiers but had in fact sought to escape the Chinese to worship God in peace. Their war stories might upset them.

"I'm afraid there is little good news to report," Lawrence began. "The Chinese have completely taken over North America and it's just a matter of time before they attain world domination. They have collapsed the dollar, so the rest of the world's currencies folded with it. The dollar was the lynchpin that held the rest of the world's economies up. But I think you're safe here. You are pretty deep in the woods with no real access. The Chinese have too much on their plates to want to bother with you."

"What about other countries' militaries? What are they doing? Are they fighting?" asked another.

"Well, initially there was some pushback from Europe, but China detonated a few nukes and threatened complete annihilation unless they agreed to a complete surrender, no different than what happened here in America. I'm hearing that Israel, Iraq, and Iran have joined together to resist. They may worship God differently, but those differences are miniscule compare to the Chinese wishing to abolish religion entirely. So far the Chinese have left them alone, but that won't last forever."

"The Chinese didn't collapse our dollar. We did that all by ourselves." Heads turned to a small, tidy, bespectacled man sitting down the far end. "As most of you know, I was a banker before the great collapse of America. I used to be a vice president of Chase Bank in Boston until my wife died and I wanted to move back to Millinocket, back to my roots, if you will. I was raised in Maine and felt fortunate to have done so. The people from this state tend to be plainspoken, straightforward, and politically conservative. Did you know that Maine has the highest percentage of personal income saved than any other state? We tend not to buy something unless we can pay for it or *need* it. You won't find too many Jaguars or Porsche car dealers up here. Not too good in the snow, too expensive to fix, and you can't haul a lot of wood or put a deer in the trunk," he chuckled.

"So you're saying it was *our* fault we got in this mess?" someone asked.

"Indirectly, yes. Let me give you an analogy. John's a plumber, married with two kids, both in grade school. Let's say his wife doesn't work to keep it simple. So John makes $35,000 a year gross. He pays taxes, and say gets to keep $30,000 of it. That money goes to pay for his mortgage, kids' clothes, maybe a car payment, a night out for pizza with the family—well, you get the picture. He puts $5,000 away for the kids' college, maybe for braces. So now he's living on $25,000. If you ask John if he's going to buy a sports car, he'd just laugh and say, 'Well, I'd *like to*, but I just can't afford it.' If you ask John if he'd like to give $4,000 to a Red Cross relief fund, he might give ten or twenty dollars, but that's all he could afford. Simple math, right? You don't have to have a PhD in economics from Harvard to understand that you can't spend more money than you earn.

"Now equally simple, but on a much, much bigger scale, is our federal government. Except they don't go to work to make any money. They don't fix broken pipes like John here. They just receive money from people by way of taxes. With this tax revenue, they are supposed to fix the roads and bridges, maintain a military for our safety, fund some higher education in schools, and make sure the meat and vegetables we buy are safe to eat. Well, you get the picture. So let's say the government receives a nice round—I'll make it low—*income* of say one hundred million dollars. They didn't earn it. That's due to the hard work of John and millions like him. That's the number, one hundred million, they have to work with, or raise more money through taxes. But instead of living within their budget like John has to, they overspend. Each senator and congressman in their district wants to build their own bridge to nowhere so they can say they are doing something for *their* people and get reelected. They get perks that are the envy of every working man and woman. The other congressmen and senators go along with it because they will want their own pet projects, which we can't afford either. They treat the treasury, which has *our* money, like one big piggy bank they can rob for anything they want. Wall Street became another Las Vegas.

"So now the one hundred million is not enough. So rather than cut out the frivolous spending of *our* money, or cutting back like all of us had to at one time or another, they borrow money from other countries, which are glad to lend it to get a piece of America. Now for the really crazy part, not only do we borrow money—lots of it—to waste in our own country, but we *give it to other countries!* That would be like John needing a new car and borrowing the money for one, but rather than buying it for his own family, *giving* it to some guy in another state! The US, before the great collapse, was *trillions of dollars in debt, yet borrowed more money just to give it to other countries!* And the worst thing of all…we let our politicians do it! What right did our government have to give our hard-earned money—money *we* earned through our sweat and labor—to either waste or give to someone else? Let the other countries take care of themselves. It'd be like some politician showing up at John's house saying he needed to borrow $10,000 to give to someone in another part of the world or buy a new sports car. You know what John would do, right? He'd throw the bum out of his house. And in summary, that's what we should have done with our politicians. Thrown *them* out! I mean, how is it *even possible* to get nineteen trillion dollars in debt?" The banker's comments set loose a flurry of opinions from those sitting around the table.

"Wow," someone said. "They always said charity begins at home, home being America. I heard a lot of the money we gave other countries just went into some dictators' pockets anyway."

"I remember reading about all the perks Congress used to get. The best health care is paid for by us, of course. Gym memberships, massages, free food, limos, trips around the world, free haircuts where the barber would come to them, and the best pension plans. No one ever offered me a free haircut. I wish I had those perks."

"You know something funny? When George Washington was elected president, Congress wouldn't even pay for his horse. They figured it was his horse, therefore his bill. Look at all the things we used to have to pay for, for these elected officials."

"One thing I never could understand is how in DC, even in the shadow of the White House, they had one of the highest murder rates and poverty levels. They couldn't even take care of the problems in their own back yards!"

"I guess it was partly our fault. When we heard those stories out of Washington we'd just shrug our shoulders like we couldn't do anything about it. We began to spend more time watching television and being distracted by these so called celebrities falling off the wagon than paying attention to what our own government was doing."

"Our politicians' desire for money and power far outweighed their commitment to God."

Matt spoke. "Jesus died to give us hope and show us the way to heaven. Only our faith and love for God can lead us through death and into eternal life. We will all appear before God, even the Chinese. They will know that the lake of fire is the ultimate destination of everything wicked. Yes, we lost America, but the kingdom of God is not a visible earthly kingdom. Know this: whether you end up in heaven or hell is not God's plan or choice, but your own. Okay, enough gloom and doom talk. God wants us to be happy and enjoy life. Rick, why don't you break out your fiddle and let's have some good music to go along with dessert!"

Far overhead, unseen and unheard by Matt, Lawrence, and the rest, a Chinese drone flew searching for them.

Fall 2028

WHITE HOUSE

GENERAL PENGYOU SUMMONED Colonel Lam, the officer in charge of the Black Tigers, to his headquarters.

"I want drone surveillance expanded over this area immediately. Make sure the aircraft fly above ten thousand feet. I want them to be virtually invisible from the ground. The target is a guerilla unit that has been attacking our remote outposts with impunity."

Pointing to a map, General Pengyou continued, "Present intel suggests that they may be in this wooded sector. Premier Chang wishes them taken alive. We have reason to believe they are operating out of a support settlement located in the same area. Once the drones have located the camp, we'll fly the WZ-10s in, then deploy our troops, blocking any possible retreat. The soldiers are to be taken alive. There will be civilians as well. The orders are that they are to be terminated. This mission is of the utmost importance and failure will not be tolerated. We launch the drones tonight with infrared cameras. I want pictures on my computer screen when they find them. Even hidden, the heat sensors should pick up their location within a few days. Once the group is located, we'll deploy immediately from here. Have your unit ready to assemble at a moment's notice. I will be accompanying you and your

172

men. We go regardless of the weather. Rations for one day only. Dismissed."

With Colonel Lam gone, General Pengyou again reviewed the information on this mission. He had to admire this rebel leader who led his soldiers. Obviously he was a highly skilled military man to operate so effectively and so long in such an unforgivable environment. He wondered what motivated him when everyone else surrendered. He hoped to have a chance to interrogate him before Chang crucified him.

Fall 2028

NORTH WOODS MAINE

THE MEN, WOMEN, and children danced under the rich blanket of the night stars. Matt and Lawrence sat contentedly, a rare state of being for either of the two men. Soon the warm fall wind will have come and gone, replaced with the frigid air of winter, but that was later. Everyone learned to live in the present, enjoying each little bit of happiness that should stumble their way. Matt leaned down and picked up a forest fern, noticing its perfection, every little delicate detail. The moon had risen now and provided a shimmering silvery light off the nearby mountains.

"I'm beat," Matt said to Lawrence. "I think I'll start moseying along to my cabin. There's plenty of room, so why don't you stay with me? This time of year tends to get a little fickle...might even rain. I have plenty of room, and I can even brew you a cup of tea if you'd like...with leaves from the forest, unfortunately. We ran out of tea bags and coffee some time ago. The leaves make a bitter brew, but you get used to it."

"Thanks, but I'm going to head down the trail head," he said, not wanting Matt to know that he constantly worried about the Chinese following their trail, no matter how careful they were. "I kinda like sleeping outdoors. My men really appreciated the clean clothes and wanted me to thank whoever scrubbed them."

"No problem. But seriously, I do want to speak to you about staying longer. Your men are exhausted, and if you were human, you would be too. We're safe here. Stay, rest, get your strength back..."

"No, but thank you. The truth is, the Chinese are looking for us and I'm afraid they won't stop until they find us. By staying here, tempting as it is, we are only putting you and your people in danger. I can't allow that. We'll stay here a day or two more, and then we'll push on. It might be a good idea if we don't meet again. I was thinking of crossing over into Canada—if we still can call it Canada, I guess. It's even more remote, and the Chinese don't have enough assets to adequately cover that amount of square miles yet. We'll be safer there."

"All right, if I can't change your mind. I certainly don't want to interfere in your business. Any of your men are more than welcome to stay, but I must ask you for a favor."

"What's that?"

"We have a young man by the name of Tom who's itching to join up with you and get back at the Chinese. I'm afraid he's influencing some of the other boys..."

"I already spoke to him. I told him there's no way either he or anyone else is joining our team. We are all professional soldiers. He'd only get killed, and probably us along with him. I expressed to him how important it was for him to remain and safeguard your camp. He was disappointed, but I think he's found a new purpose."

"Thanks, Lawrence. Good night. I'll head to my cabin and see you in the morning."

"Good night, Matt. Sleep well."

Lawrence shouldered his rifle and, checking his compass, went off the trail, heading toward the nearest mountain. There was a full moon out, making it possible to navigate through the forest. The sounds of nightly predators began to make their presence known—coyotes on the prowl, and birds of prey in the air. Lawrence hiked for a mile or more without breaking a sweat. He occasionally came across a deer, but standing still he became invisible even to the animals in their own habitat. The night hours crept along as he made his way first to the base of the mountain and then began his ascent. He climbed steadily until he reached a vantage point where he had fairly good visibility of the forest beneath him. Some smoke trails still rose from Matt's camp, which gave his stomach a nervous rumble. He heard an owl perched in a tree nearby, and it was only by chance, turning his head in that direction, that he saw the drone silhouetted against the moonlight. He watched the ultimate predator cruise by his position, heading for the lights of the campfires of the settlement. He slipped off his rifle, holding the scope up to his eye, and he could see that it was a Chinese drone, no mistaking it. He could only hope that the drone's operator was asleep or not paying attention to the images the drone was sending back, but when it passed over the campsite, then turned for another pass, that slight hope vanished. An icy finger curled around his heart as he realized that the Chinese had found the camp. He and his men could escape into the woods, but it would be impossible to move that many women and children to safety. He quickly repositioned his rifle back on his shoulder, tightened his backpack firmly against his body, and proceeded to march double time through the woods back to the camp to sound the alarm.

The thought that he had led the Chinese to their encampment lay heavy on his mind.

As Lawrence was hiking through the woods to reach the mountain, Matt went back to his cabin. He sat out on the front porch, now one side tipping heavily toward the ground, and put his butt down on the top wooden step. He undid the laces on his well-worn boots, letting them fall to the ground. He sat alone with his thoughts. It had begun to rain softly, and he watched the raindrops begin to drip silently off the roof of his cabin. Each tiny raindrop would take a moment to fall, hanging on to the roof as if fighting the inevitable plunge to the ground. When it could no longer hold its weight, it slipped off the edge. *How like us*, Matt thought. The years adding to our weight until it became time to let go. The motion of the raindrops, slowly forming and falling, mesmerized Matt, putting him into a fugue state. Somewhere off in the distance he heard his name being called, not in the direction of the village, but deeper in the woods. His eyes searched for the sound until off in the distance, through the towering and wide pine trees, he saw his father.

"Dad?" he called, shaking his head, his eyes not believing what they saw. "Dad? Is that really you? But how…" He stepped off his porch, so fixed on the vision in front of him that he didn't feel the rocks pinch the soles of his naked feet. He walked to his father, who was looking at him, smiling but motionless. He appeared to be backlit by a shimmering bluish white light which enveloped his body. Matt rubbed his eyes not knowing if this was a dream. When he was within feet of his father, he stopped. The experience was so disorienting, he froze.

"Son, you must listen very carefully to me. At dawn tomorrow, when the sun rises over the mountain, you must lead your people out of this place. You must take enough food for forty days and forty nights, but no more. You must not take any weapons, only tools and provisions to sustain you. You will head west on a path that will be revealed to you. You will come to an old abandoned mine. The sign resting on the rusted iron door will say Iron Mountain. The door will be locked and rusted shut, but when you touch it, it will open. You must lead your people into the mine and then shut the door. You must stay within the cave for forty days and forty nights. Do not leave until the door opens, then all will be revealed to you."

"Dad, is it really you?" Tears began to fall down his cheeks as his eyes filled. "I miss you, Dad. You left without ever saying good-bye."

"I'm with you, son. I have always been with you. Someday, when it's your mother's and your time, we'll be united again in heaven for all eternity."

"Why, Dad? Why me? What if the people don't believe me? What will happen? I'm afraid, Dad."

"Do not be afraid, son. Do you remember our fishing trip on your eighth birthday? God came to you with a special task, a task you have been preparing for your whole life. This is that task, son, and this is that day. You must lead your people to safety, as there will be a terrible reckoning on Earth as God passes His final judgment, removing the wickedness from His people. As it was written and foretold, it will come to pass. The day of the great apocalypse is upon us. Now you must do what God asks of you, as you always have, my son."

"Dad...."

"I'm must go now, Matt. Prepare your people. We will all meet in the glory of the kingdom of heaven someday."

Matt's father turned and walked away, his long, lean body still clothed in farmer's overalls and boots not quite touching the ground. As he walked, his body luminescence began to fade until his apparition was no more.

Matt sat stunned on the wet pine needles. This time, unlike when he was eight, he knew exactly what had happened. Whether it was truly his father or the Holy Ghost that appeared to him, he didn't know, but the message was crystal clear—the second coming of Jesus was at hand, and mankind would pay for its wicked ways. Surprisingly, he felt no fear. No apprehension. Somehow he had been preparing for this day all his life. Now he must go to his people and prepare them for this great journey. As he stood up, he became instantly aware of something different.

For the first time since he was eight, he was no longer cold.

Lawrence

NORTH WOODS

H E RAN DOWN the mountain through the heavy brush, ignoring the sharp branches that tore at his skin and scratched his eyes. He stumbled twice, then tumbled to the ground. He twisted his body as he fell in an attempt to avoid a protruding rock. He heard a crack as his cheek hit the rock, and realized he had knocked out a tooth. Bleeding profusely, he ignored the pain. He knew he had to evacuate the settlers, since the drone had detected their location, but to where? He was fully aware of the efficiency and ruthlessness of the Chinese military. He was racked with guilt that their search for him might have led them to Matt's group. *What's done is done,* he thought. He now needed to convince Matt and his people that they had to abandon their settlement which was the only home they'd known for the past few years.

He knew the map of the area by heart. Because Matt had flooded all the roads and waterways south of his position, it would be likely the Chinese would have to air drop their soldiers in to the north and then hike in on foot. He doubted they would drop directly into the village, as they would be sitting ducks to Lawrence's guns. The smart move would be to drop in a secure opening, then seal off the area and flank them on both sides. They could just as easily bomb the settlement, but the Chinese were all about making examples. While he didn't fear for his men—they were soldiers—he grimaced at the thought of what the Chinese would do to the civilians.

As he accelerated his pace into a full-blown sprint, the pine trees became a blur. He rounded a bend, and the village came in sight. It appeared that Matt had convened a meeting. The settlers were seated in a circle on the ground, and Matt stood in the middle. Matt looked different somehow. Lawrence slowed down and walked past the outermost huts. He approached the group and listened in rapt attention to Matt's every word.

"Gather enough food for your family for forty days. We will *not* take any weapons. Bring warm clothes, but we must leave most of our possessions here. Perhaps we will come back and retrieve them. I can't guarantee that, though. The second coming of Jesus is upon us. Instead of being afraid, let us rejoice. For our faith has made us among the chosen people to survive. I somehow know there are pockets of people like us all over the world that will also be saved. Go back to your cabins, pack, and try to get some rest. We move at first light."

The settlers rose from the ground and walked slowly back to their cabins. There were no discussions, no dissent or outbursts. They all had seen that something had changed in Matt, that somehow he was filled with a divine light. They went about the task of gathering food with calm efficiency. Mothers and fathers hugged their children and each other.

"What's going on?" Lawrence asked Matt. "You're hurt." Lawrence wiped away the blood from his mouth on the back of his sleeve and dismissed the question.

"Matt, what's going on?" He waited for Matt's response, thinking he had possibly had seen the drone too. But where were they planning to go?

"Lawrence, this may seem somewhat crazy to you, but I can assure you I'm very serious. When I was a boy, I had a vision that someday I would be called upon to complete a task. A task given by God. Just a little while ago, I was told to gather my people and leave camp at first light. I am to take my people to a safe place, an abandoned mine, where we are to remain for forty days and nights. It's the End of Days, Lawrence. Whether you choose to believe me or not, I beseech you to come with us. Even if you don't believe, you will have lost nothing."

"Matt, right now all I know is that I spotted a Chinese drone, looking for me, no doubt. You'll never make it to where you're going. Their paratroopers are most likely being deployed as we speak."

"God will protect us. We are to go to an abandoned mine called Iron Mountain."

"*If* you make it to where you're going. You won't. I know where Iron Mountain is. It's at least a full day's hike, and the Chinese will be hot on your tail. They'll drop in behind you and chase you down. You'll never make it."

"Lawrence, please don't worry about the Chinese. Their Day of Judgment is at hand. Please, lay down your arms and have your men do the same. Join us in welcoming the second coming of our Lord."

"My men will be packed and ready to follow you, but we'll be taking our guns. They might come in handy should we get caught by the Chinese. You go get some rest Matt; you have a long hike ahead of you. I'll meet you here at the meeting point in the morning. Good night."

Lawrence watched him walk off. There was something noticeably different about him. He was *serene*. That might change tomorrow.

THE NEXT MORNING

NOT ONE SETTLER got a wink of sleep by the time dawn came. Just as they had done when driven out of their homes in Millinocket, they had quickly assembled the required bags of food, clothes, and supplies. Their faces were solemn but resolute. Almost wordlessly they went to the communal table and took their seats, nodding in silent resignation to their neighbors.

Lawrence had assembled his men down at the trailhead. "The Chinese are coming. The drone gave up our position last night, and their paratroopers are no doubt in the air as we speak. I'm afraid it doesn't look good for us. We've banded together in a singular mission of hunt and destroy, but we all knew this day would come. So I'm freeing you from your mission. You are free to pursue whatever course you like. If you slip out now, westbound, there's a good chance you'll slip through the Chinese lines. It's just too wooded for them to have any line of sight to cover it all. I don't care how many men they deploy."

"What about them?" a man asked, looking at the massed group.

"Honestly? They don't have a chance. There's too many of them to get to the mine before the Chinese roll up on them. I spoke to Matt about keeping their guns, but he was adamant that this was not going to happen. You and

I know I'd rather die in a firefight than be captured by those butchers. I wish I had his faith."

"What are you going to do, Lawrence?"

"I'm going to follow them. The only place the Chinese can parachute in without getting hung up in the trees is at this junction point," he answered, indicating an area with a small clearing. "From there, they'll make good time catching up. Matt has too many women and children to make any time. They'll slow him down. I figure Matt will almost make it to within a quarter mile to the entrance to the mine before he's overrun. I'm going to stay at his rear and try to hold the Chinese off and buy him a little time."

"It's a suicide mission, Lawrence. I doubt you'll be able to hold them off by yourself, so I'm going to join you. You gotta die someday, right?"

The other three men looked at each other and smiled. "Right. We're in. Let's show those Chinese how some real soldiers fight."

Lawrence looked at his men and nodded. He expected no less, but his heart swelled with pride. "Okay. We'll follow Matt until he reaches this point here," indicating a boulder crop that they would have to pass through in order to reach the mine. We'll take up positions on either side, let the Chinese get halfway through, and catch them in a crossfire, which will give Matt plenty of time to make it to the mine head. God help them if they can't get in. We need to secure every bit of ammo they are planning on leaving behind, and a few more guns if they're a different caliber. Better sharpen your knives; I have a feeling the fighting may get hand to hand. Okay, men. Our last mission. Let's grab that ammo and join Matt. He'll lead the way, and we'll hang back to protect his flank. God be with you men. See you on the other side."

Matt had assembled his people in small groups, women and children toward the front so they wouldn't lag behind, and men at the front and rear. He checked every backpack to ensure the younger members didn't violate the order on weapons. When he was satisfied, he gave the order to move out. He had a few of the older men at the head of the line, and they proceeded to move into the heart of the forest along the path Matt indicated. One foot in front of the other, they walked forward toward their destiny.

"So, are you going to join us, Lawrence?" Matt asked, seeing Lawrence and his men in full battle attire and lingering behind.

"No. We'll follow you for a little while and make sure you get there, and then we'll be heading west. This will be the end of the line, Matt. I wish you well."

"It doesn't have to end this way, Lawrence."

"I think it does. You have your destiny and we have ours. I think by protecting your butt we may actually buy a little salvation, Matt. We'll stay with you until you're safe and sound. Let's just get you to the mine and then we'll see, okay?"

"Okay. Just keep an open mind."

"I will, my friend."

They had hiked for the better part of the day, crossing the open clearing an hour earlier when the sky was suddenly filled with white floating parachutes gliding gently toward the ground. Lawrence watched impassionedly and summoned one of his men to bring Matt to the rear. "You need to push your people. You're still a mile from the mine shaft head and need to move. The Chinese will be on the ground in a few minutes, and they could reach this position within the hour. We're going to hang back and welcome them to Maine."

"Come with us. We can make it together."

"No, we won't. The only place we can stop them is that small sway back there. It gives us some advantage being in the rocky outcrop above them. Anywhere else, they'll be able to catch us quickly. We can put them in a bottleneck. You guys go, we'll catch up later. We'll be fine."

Matt looked into Lawrence's eyes and saw the lie. They wouldn't be catching up. They would be sacrificing their lives to allow Matt's people to get to the mine. He leaned over and started to shake Lawrence's hand, but instead pulled him into his chest and hugged him. "God will bless you, Lawrence. You and your men."

"You just get going, and we'll talk about it later tonight. Maybe over a couple of beers and some fresh hot meat pies. Now get."

Lawrence twirled his right finger in the air, and he and his men reversed their course and headed back down the trail. When they came to the rocky outcrop, he sent two men on high to both the left and right sides. "You wait until I fire. Let them get halfway up and we'll catch them in cross-fire. That'll knock down some of their numbers, but judging by the amount of chutes I saw, it'll only be a matter of time before they go around and flank us." Lawrence looked around at his men and smiled. "I've never been prouder to serve than with you men. You know we Kiwis love a good fight—now let's go kick some Chinese butt."

The men picked their way up through the boulders, giving themselves enough separation that the narrow canyon would be entirely in their gun sights. Lawrence walked to the head of the canyon and sat down in between two large craggy boulders. He checked the action on his gun and pulled his killing knife from his vest, putting it in his belt, and sat back. He looked but could not see his men. He glanced at the sky, cloudless, and felt the breeze on his face. He was calm in the face of his death. "I'm coming home, Amy," he whispered as he thought of her smiling face. All the longing he had tried to hold back all these long, tiring years reached a crescendo, and his chest heaved with his loss. He could feel Amy tugging on his ear, kissing his cheek, her voice whispering to come home to her. It was time.

A squad of Chinese troops marching as quickly as the terrain allowed appeared one hundred yards out, heading straight into the canyon. Lawrence coldly watched them approach. The man leading them was older, but lean and hard, marching fast. He had the four red stars on his shoulders that a Chinese general would wear. *Wow,* thought Lawrence, *they really sent out the big guns for us.* He waited until half of them picked their way through the pass, oblivious to Lawrence and his men, marching without fear, and then Lawrence stood up, leaving the safety of the rocks, and said loud enough for both the Chinese and his men to hear, "Hello, you godless butchers! You looking for us?" Then, gripping his automatic machine gun on his hip, he unleashed a deadly spray of bullets, spewing fire and lead, catching both the general and the men behind him, their mouths still open in surprise. His men jumped up from both sides, firing maniacally into the confused soldiers. The Chinese beat a hasty retreat, those who could, allowing Lawrence and his men time to reload. The Chinese, too many for this small, brave band of brothers, began to swing wide up the hill and flank his soldiers on both sides. The fighting was furious, the air pockmarked with screams of injured and dying men, until finally, only silence. With the Chinese general killed, the next commanding officer yelled to Lawrence, "Your men are dead. Surrender and we'll spare your life. Our orders are to take you alive. You will not be harmed. You will be put in prison for your crimes."

Lawrence could hear the Chinese soldiers picking their way through the rocks, surrounding him. He knew it was over.

"What promises do I have that I will not be harmed?"

"You have my word, as colonel of the Black Tigers."

"Then I will only surrender to you. No other. You must come alone, as I don't trust one of your men to get an itchy trigger finger."

"Okay. Put your gun down, and don't shoot or my men will cut you down." He was pleased that *he* would be the one bringing in the elusive and deadly White Ghost. What a promotion he would receive! The captain walked out of his hiding place fifty yards in front of Lawrence and walked toward him. He had his Chinese machine gun at the ready, but had a disarming smile on his face. As he walked up to Lawrence, he said, "You and your men fought bravely. I think you'll find that we will treat you fairly…"

"Fairly? How's this for fair? You killed my wife." With that, Lawrence grabbed the muzzle of the machine gun, its bullets flying harmlessly into the ground, and plunged his knife into the captain's heart. "That's for Amy."

Lawrence never felt any of the hundred bullets that ripped apart his body. His last vision was of his smiling Amy welcoming him into her arms.

Matt stopped when he heard the gunfire." Quick, quick," he yelled. His people broke into a panic as they raced to the cave that was barred by a heavy, rusted iron door. A *No Trespassing* sign hung sideways beneath an even older sign saying *IRON MOUNTAIN,* its letters faded and cracked. The few at the front, seeing the entrance blocked, began to weep as they looked over their shoulders, hearing the screams of the dying men. They tugged and pulled at the handle, but the door wouldn't budge. One man began to pound on it with his fist. Matt strode up to the door and placed his hand against it, feeling the rust grind into his skin. A loud groan was emitted from deep inside the mine shaft, like a prehistoric animal being awakened rudely from its slumber. The door creaked open a crack, then with a thunderous bang, flew open, smashing against the opposite wall.

"Now! Everyone into the mine. Quickly! We haven't a lot of time." Men, women, and children scrambled into the mine and to safety. Matt stood by the iron door, guiding everyone in, but looking back on the trail hoping against hope and reason that Lawrence and his men made it. The realization that they sacrificed their lives so Matt's people could live slowly and painful washed over him. He yelled in the cave, making certain that everyone had made it. He quickly entered and began to panic, not knowing how to close the door, when on its own the door began to move— slowly at first, then slamming shut.

They were safe.

DEEP IN IRON MOUNTAIN

WHEN THE IRON door clanged shut, the heavy metallic noise reverberated ominously throughout the cave. Matt and his family huddled near the door, anxiously worrying whether the Chinese soldiers would be able to breach this barrier and reach them. The screams of fighting men penetrated the walls, then gave way to the anguished cries and moans of the dying. That too eventually came to a deafening quiet. Everyone silently acknowledged that Lawrence and his men had made the ultimate sacrifice. They had given their lives for the freedom of the others. Their hearts were heavy as they reflected on the bravery of those who had defended them.

After waiting long hours for the assault that never materialized, Matt and George told the rest of the family they were safe and to wait for them there while they explored the cave. The first thing they noticed was the ambient light. The ceilings and walls were coated with natural phosphorus that came to life while the cave door was open, allowing daylight to penetrate for the first time in years. Matt remembered hearing that Iron Mountain was an old mining site that had been closed decades ago when the demand for quartz diminished. Off to the side lay a rusted rail car. Old, faded signs hung on the cave's wall prohibiting smoking or fires of any kind due to the risk of explosions by the collecting gases.

Matt and George walked deeper, still in silence, each of them trying to assess their predicament. The cave opened up into a larger cavern, almost forty feet square, that then tapered off into tunnels that ran deeper into the earth. There were warning signs posted near the entrance to the tunnels that advised all who entered to wear hard hats and carry safety rope. Off to one side, a pool of water had formed in a rock fissure, being fed by an unseen underground stream.

George leaned over and cupped the water, then brought it up to his nose. "Smells okay." Then he dripped a few drops on his tongue. "As sweet as any water I've ever tasted." Both men gave exhausted smiles, knowing the lifesaving importance of their discovery.

"God provides," Matt said tiredly. "Let's get the rest of the group and move them in here."

They walked upwards back to the front of the cavern where the rest of the group sat huddled by the still-shut iron door. Faces were filled with questions and apprehension. "We found fresh water deeper in the mine, and a larger cavern where we can spread out," George announced.

"How long will we be here, and what if the Chinese come back?" someone asked.

"They won't," Matt answered. "We're safe now. God gave us His promise. We are about to witness the second coming of Christ. His angel told me we are to remain here for forty days and forty nights. I fear and pray for the sinners and unbelievers who have brought down His wrath. It is prophesied that the Second Coming will be by fire. God will cleanse His earth of wickedness by scorching it, but we will remain safe here."

"Will there be other survivors?"

"I don't know, but I must believe that other true believers such as ourselves will also be saved."

"Matt, what if you're wrong? What if we're trapped in here just waiting for the Chinese to come back, or we run out of food and water?" a panicked man asked.

"We are the new children of Abraham. And like Abraham we were tested time and time again. Just as Joseph and Mary were chosen to bear Jesus, we and people like us were chosen to reaffirm the relationship between man and God. Who created the earth, the sea, and the skies? God did. Yes, it's scary. The angel of death is coming, swooping down on the sinners and nonbelievers with the Lord's fury, but God will protect us in this darkest hour."

Matt walked over to one of the large duffle bags and pulled out two loaves of bread. He asked the group to gather around. He broke a piece of the crusted loaf and passed the remaining piece. Each person knew the significance of this act, as old as when Jesus broke bread with His disciples. When each had a piece, with heads bowed, Matt led them in prayer.

The cave grew brighter, and their faith in God's love replaced the fear in their hearts.

GOD'S FINAL JUDGMENT

*When the End of Days arrives, and man
sits in final judgment, With it comes
eternal life for those who are saved.*

XI CHANG SAT at his desk, waiting anxiously for a report from General Pengyou. Although Xi had demanded radio silence throughout the operation, he was apprehensive about the general's failure to contact him. The suspense of finally capturing the White Ghost gave him a bout of nervous excitement and would signal the end of the militia opposition.

He was looking out of the open french doors that led to the balcony when he was startled by the sound of clamorous trumpets blaring from the heavens above—so loud and all encompassing, the sound completely enveloped the White House. Chang instinctively put his hands over his ears to prevent his eardrums from bursting. He tilted his head trying to comprehend the origin of the most unusual, unrelenting sound. He leaped from his chair and sprinted outside. In the sky before him, a mass of clouds both majestic and menacing blotted out the daytime sky and rolled toward him. He stood breathless, unable to move as he witnessed this celestial event. The forward movement of the clouds stopped, and from the center of the white mass, God, surrounded by His angels, revealed His wrathful face to Chang. The voice of God spoke directly to Chang:

> *"It is so written that if any man worshipped the beast he shall drink of the wine of My wrath, and he shall be tormented by the fires of hell in the presence of the Lamb. And the smoke of their torment shall ascend up forever and ever to the heavens, and they shall have no rest day or night, for that is the eternal punishment for those who worship the beast."*

With those words, God pointed His hand and extended His finger downward to the depths of hell, and pulled the earth open and unleashed an unholy fireball and thrust it toward Chang.

A horrific ball of fire rose in the sky, growing larger with its ascension. It appeared to be *moving,* growing larger even still, as it was heading directly for him. He was mesmerized by the sight, unable to look away from the incandescent yellow orb increasing in size right before his eyes. Giant flames violently erupted from its center. As it flew toward him, traveling miles in just moments, the intense heat set his hair ablaze and blistered his skin. Closer now, he could see hundreds—no, thousands—of writhing bodies, twisting and turning in intense anguish, their silent screams shrouded in the liquid fire. The inferno almost upon him, he could see the devil clearly now, his obscene, long, red-forked tongue flickering in and out of his serpent's mouth. As Chang's skin cracked and melted, exposing naked muscles and ligaments, he could now see the devil's tail, comprised of a hundred or more terrifying snakes intertwined, fangs extended. The large, curled horns of a ram sprouted from the devil's skull, blood oozing from its base. In a second, it was on him. Just before hell opened to consume him, he was aware of his screams.

On that day, as foretold in the Bible, God turned man's sins into a holy fire, burning away all the evil that man had brought into His Garden of Eden. His weapons of war—devastating nuclear bombs, with the sole purpose to kill—exploded in their bunkers and in the military vehicles that housed them. A terrifying, massive flood of flames and molten lava flowed over the earth's surface, killing sinners and nonbelievers alike, and purifying everything in its path. Plumes of fire reached out to the heavens, blackening the skies and plunging the earth into terrifying darkness. Fish died in the seas, and the birds fell from the sky. Violent earthquakes split open the land, swallowing everything that lay before it. Winds unleashed from the four corners of the world accelerated a great cleansing fire that swept and purified the Earth.

God called to His angels as He fulfilled His prophecy of divine judgment.

Epilogue

IRON MOUNTAIN

THE DAYS PASSED slowly for the Christians locked in Iron Mountain. It was quiet inside save the sounds of a terrible storm which raged outside their door. They prayed every day and gave thanks to God for allowing them to flee the Chinese in safety, and for the brave souls of Lawrence and his men who laid down their lives in sacrifice. When someone asked why God would exact such a high price from these good men, Matt simply said it was all in God's plan, but he had no doubt that each of the men was now basking in the Lord's light free from the earthly pain and suffering. Now they were in heaven with their loved ones who had passed before them.

The family ate sparingly, both from a diminished lack of appetite and also to make their rations last the forty days Matt said they would have to remain locked away from the rest of the world. The children, being children, quickly adapted to their new environment, playing games of catch when not exploring the cave under the watchful eyes of their parents. On one such outing, one of the young men discovered ancient cave paintings of men hunting and praying. This cave art raised the family's spirits, seeing how even prehistoric man knew that there was a higher power than themselves.

At dinner time, Matt began every meal by gathering everyone around in a circle. From God's endless bounty, the sack holding the bread was always replenished no matter how much was eaten. After breaking off a piece of bread, he passed it around in remembrance of Jesus's sacrifice taking away the sins of the world. Then Matt offered a prayer before supper began. When they finished eating, the children clamored for the adults to sing songs to them. Of course, the children's favorites were Christmas carols. Not one person complained of any hardship.

When Tom, who was given the job of recording the days passed by scratching a line with a sharp stone on the cave walls, indicated that in just two days they would have been there for the forty Matt predicted, a collective nervous emotion arose. Would the heavy iron door open? What would remain outside? Would the storm they heard end? Were there any other survivors? Matt remained calm, reminding them of their bond with God and not to worry.

In the early morning of the fortieth day, when most were still sleeping, the door opened.

After Matt and his family spent forty days and forty nights locked deep within the earth's bosom, praying by candlelight, praising God with all His blessings, they were suddenly startled by the sound of the heavy iron door at the mouth of Iron Mountain, its massive rusty hinges creaking open.

One by one, led by Matt, they shielded their eyes against the brilliant sunlight that now filled the mine. Temporarily blinded by the light, they stepped out into a barren, desolate landscape. Everywhere as far as their eyes could see, the landscape was charred and blackened. Smoke arose from numerous small fires still burning. No sign of life existed, not flora nor fauna. Clouds of black dust swirled high over their heads. No sounds of life could be heard. Only silence.

The settlers, firm in their faith and love of God, instead of cursing their new predicament or wringing their hands and crying, gave thanks for sparing them His Wrath. The Wrath of God. As they looked out into the barren, blackened crusted fields, a single flower began to grow, then another and another. Sprouts of grass rapidly spread across the once-barren fields, now painting it shades of green. A spring with clear blue water sprung out of the ground, filling a basin with a new lake. Fish began to jump in the water, splashing and making their presence known. Massive trees erupted out of the ground, forming a new forest. The sky was filled with golden sunshine. A robin began its song. Animals of the forest began to appear. Deer, bears, moose, foxes, and squirrels began their new beginnings. The black swirls of dust turned into white, puffy clouds, sprinkling blue-green water drops here and there. Life began anew.

The world was reborn.

Someone pointed and said, "Look." Off in the near distance, there appeared an apple orchard, filled with bounty but also with a man with a loving smile surrounded by a white shimmering light. Someone asked Matt to go to him, thinking it must be another vision meant for him, but Matt said, "No, we shall all go together."

They walked together holding hands and entered the orchard. Matt knew immediately that this time, this was not his father before him—perhaps it never was. Every member of the family, from the very old to the very young, knew they were in the presence of Jesus, yet no one was afraid. One small boy went forward and touched His white robe. Jesus smiled and, touching the boy on his head, said,

"Do not be afraid. This is the Second Coming that was foretold in the Bible. My Father in heaven unleashed a great fire that swept away all of man's wickedness. Your faith saved you and other people scattered across the Earth as well. He gave you a new life, free from corruption and evil." Turning to Matt, He said, "In your hand you hold your family's Bible, My Holy Book. Follow its teachings; it will be the only guide you need to enter the kingdom of heaven which My Father has prepared for you, where life is eternal. He has restored life on Earth as it was meant to be. Fill your hearts with love, as My Father loves you. Go forth and multiply the Earth. Live in peace. You have a new beginning."

Jesus smiled and said, "I must go now, but I will always be with you in your song and in your prayers. Keep Holy the Sabbath and you will enter the kingdom of heaven, and eternal life will be yours."

With that, Jesus turned and walked away through the orchard until He was out of sight.

Matt dropped to his knees and, looking upward, thanked God.

The End

ABOUT THE AUTHOR

J IM BALZOTTI HAS written more than twenty books on horseback riding and dude ranches. He's appeared on *Good Morning America* and *Horseman's Radio Weekly*, and written for *Western Horseman*. Born and raised in East Boston and a graduate of Amherst College, Jim today travels between the Florida's Treasure Coast and Maine, accompanied by Chopper, his German Shepherd.

CONTACT THE AUTHOR

jim@wrathofgod.com